# DEADLY
# REMEDIES

A police doctor hunts a serial killer

## CANDY DENMAN

Paperback edition published by

The Book Folks

London, 2021

ISBN  978-1-913516-36-9

www.thebookfolks.com

*DEADLY REMEDIES is the fifth novel in a series of medical crime fiction titles featuring police doctor Callie Hughes. More information about the other five books can be found at the end of this one.*

# Prologue

*It felt as if a river of fire was running up her arm. She cried out in pain and tried to pull away, but she couldn't move, her arm was held in too tight a grip. Her fingers clawed and her body spasmed, legs kicking uncontrollably as the pain shot towards her racing heart. It reached its destination and felt as if her chest was exploding. She gasped, eyes shooting wide, looking her killer in the eye, pleading for help as her heart stopped beating. And then it was over. Her body relaxed, the light in her eyes faded. Finally, she was at peace.*

*The killer took the time to pay respects and make the old woman look more comfortable, sat her straight in the chair, pulled her skirt down where it had ridden up and put her hat back on her head. Then, with a final check that everything was in its place, they were gone.*

# Chapter 1

It was a bizarre scene in front of her; there was no denying it.

The elderly lady was sitting in an upright, chintz-covered, wing chair, of the sort that Callie Hughes' grandmother used to have. Her hands were resting loosely in her lap. Her short grey hair had been recently permed, and what could be seen looked neatly combed under the well-worn pink felt hat. Beneath the brim her eyes were open, eyelids drooping slightly, and, using a gloved finger, Callie lifted one. The iris was a washed-out blue and the large pupil showed a hint of filminess, suggesting either incipient cataracts or that she had been dead more than a few hours and her corneas were drying out.

Bending down to get a closer look, Callie could see the woman's handbag was on the floor next to her feet, ready to be picked up. Her narrow skirt had kept her knees together, like ladies were taught to sit, and she had smart, shiny court shoes on her feet, not the comfortable house shoes that she would have been wearing if she was staying at home. There was a small dressing on the outside of her right ankle. With sadness, Callie noticed a ladder in her tights, the one flaw in her perfect turnout. She must have snagged them at the last minute and hadn't had time to change them before – well, before she died. The woman looked for all the world like she was about to go to church, for a funeral perhaps. Just not for her own.

Callie stood up. Tall and slim, shoulder-length blonde hair neatly tied back, she held her hands away from her side, anxious not to contaminate the scene or her clothes. Employed as a forensic physician by the local police force, she knew how to assess every scene and look for clues as to whether any death was natural, or not. She looked around the room and tried to block out the angry voices outside as she slowly took in the scene, trying to work out why Angus had asked her to come. Besides the obvious reason that it was all a bit strange.

There was nothing else in the room to give a clue as to what had happened here: no pill bottles, alcohol, or suicide note in open sight. Having gently checked that the old lady really was dead, Callie went back outside to interrupt the argument and speak to the doctor who had called her and the community nurse who had found the body.

"This is totally ridiculous," the nurse was telling Angus as Callie came out of the house. "I have better things to do than hang around here. My other patients are still alive and need my help."

Angus McPhail was very tall and thin and almost looked as if he could tie himself in knots when he was anxious, as he seemed to be at the moment. He was a laughable contrast to the short, stocky and, right now, rather belligerent woman who was speaking to him. Callie recognised her and was wracking her brains for a name. Judy? Julie? She didn't seem to be wearing the obligatory name tag that would have helped.

"If you could possibly just–?" Angus was as polite and ineffectual as he always was and his request made absolutely no difference to the nurse's decision. She headed firmly towards her car, which was parked further along the narrow street.

"Just a moment," Callie called loudly, with an air of authority. The woman turned with a scowl. Callie tried to ignore the curtains twitching in several of the neighbouring houses and continued in a quieter tone, "If you could tell me what happened? When you found the lady?"

The woman gave a sigh. It was clear she felt hard done by, but she returned and answered Callie.

"I come and see Mrs Mount twice a week, to dress her leg ulcer. It's almost healed." She glanced at Angus as if expecting him to refute this. "But this morning she didn't answer the door and when I let myself in, I found her, like that." She pointed in the general direction of the house.

"And is it always you who visits?"

"Yes, except when I'm on holiday or whatever."

Callie nodded her understanding.

"And she doesn't have any other help, as far as you know?"

The nurse shrugged.

"She cares for herself, generally, I think. Those stairs are a death-trap, though," she said, glaring at the doctor as if it was his fault. "Old people like her shouldn't be allowed to live in houses like that; one day she'll fall down them." The nurse seemed to suddenly remember that her patient was dead and so unlikely to do that anymore.

"Thank you, and you say she was okay the last time you saw her?"

"Well, yes, last week, as all right as she ever is, that is." She looked at Callie and explained, "She has dementia."

"Mild dementia," Angus cut in. "Pretty good for her age, otherwise."

"Not so mild, if you ask me. Last Friday she told me not to come this week because she was going away on holiday. As if that was likely. Who was supposed to be taking her, I ask you?"

Callie glanced back into the tiny fisherman's cottage where the old lady had lived. Sure enough, there was a small suitcase by the door. Not a modern wheelie bag, but an old-fashioned, cream-coloured plastic one. It looked as if it dated from the 1950s or so, but it was in pristine condition and not well used. Mrs Mount had certainly thought she was going away, and it wasn't something that happened often.

"Does she have a key-safe box?" Callie asked.

"Yes, it's on the front door, there." She gestured, and Callie could see it. "When she didn't answer, I just let myself in and found her, just as you saw. I didn't touch her or anything. I rang my manager and he told me to stay put and called the doctor. I even waited until he arrived." The nurse continued as she jerked her head at Angus, "I've done all I can. Now can I please get on? I've got more people to see."

Callie couldn't think of any reason why not, so she nodded.

"And thank you for staying until I got here," she added to the woman's retreating back. A car with some marking and a phone number on the side stopped in the narrow street and the driver wound down his window to speak to the nurse, nodding at the open door of the house.

"She's not going anywhere," she said brusquely and carried on her way. The driver started to wind up his window.

"Just a minute!" Callie called to him and he waited as she hurried over. "Were you booked to collect Mrs Mount?" she asked him.

"Yeah, well, I was told to pick up an old dear and take her to the bus station," he said. "Dunno the name, but the nurse said she ain't going."

"No, I'm sorry, she won't be."

"All the same these old buggers, don't know what day of the week it is."

"She died," Callie informed him, coldly.

"Oh." The driver looked as if he might say more, but changed his mind; if there was no passenger, there was no money and he had better things to do no doubt, so he drove away.

Callie turned and walked back to Angus. He was staring at the nurse as she headed down the street towards her car.

"Tell me what's on your mind, Angus," she said gently.

"I don't think I can sign the death certificate," he said, anxiety coming off him in waves.

"Well, if you haven't seen her in the last couple of weeks and you don't know the cause of death, that's perfectly reasonable."

His shoulders dropped and he visibly relaxed.

"Of course."

"You need to call the coroner's officer and he'll organise the removal. Are there any relatives that you know of?"

"No. I don't know." He was fidgeting again and looking anxious.

"Why did you call me?"

She hoped that if she continued to be cool and professional, as she always was, he might calm down a bit. There was definitely something worrying him.

"Because I thought it might be a crime scene," he explained. "But I wasn't sure, so—" he tailed off, unsure what to say next.

Callie went over what she had seen, but strange as it was, she couldn't understand what had made Angus think it was a crime scene. An old lady had died, possibly from the stress or excitement of going on holiday. There didn't seem to be any crime involved.

"Why?" she asked. "It's a rather strange sight, I grant you, but there was nothing there to suggest to me that she died of anything other than natural causes. What made you think it was different?"

"Because it's not the first one," he said.

# Chapter 2

Having called Mike Parton, the coroner's officer, and secured the small, terraced house, Callie led Angus to a café on the High Street. Mike was going to meet them there before going to the house.

"So, tell me what you meant by this not being the first one," she said once they were settled with their coffee.

"Caroline, my wife," Angus began unnecessarily explaining to Callie, who knew very well that Angus was married to Caroline Stratton, and that she was also a local GP. Callie could sympathise with Caroline's decision not to work in the same surgery as her husband; his constant dithering and insecurity must be bad enough at home without having to deal with it at work too.

"Caroline told me a couple of weeks ago about being called to visit a patient up in Ore who had been found dead by his carer. She told me how spooky it was to find the man, sitting in a chair, all dressed in his best clothes as if he were just waiting to go out, suitcase by the door."

Callie had to agree that it was a strange enough occurrence once, but twice was off the scale. She could understand why Angus had called her. As a police doctor, as they used to be called, she would be the person best able to advise him. Of course, most GPs in his position would just have called out the coroner's officer, but with Angus's chronic lack of self-belief, he needed someone to reassure him that that was the right course of action.

"Can you give me the details of the first patient?" she asked him.

He looked embarrassed.

"I tried to find out for you already, but Caroline's in surgery and won't take my calls. She doesn't, not unless it's something to do with the children. Something life or death, I mean. We have a code that I text her for something like that, but I'm not allowed to use it unless…" He trailed off, obviously realising that he didn't need to tell her all this.

Callie raised an eyebrow. Caroline must have got an awful lot of calls from her husband in the past, probably asking for advice on his patients, to reassure him he was doing the right tests or for her to make a decision on their treatment, and she had learned that the only way to get through her own work was to ban calls from him. It seemed harsh, but she could understand it. He really was maddening.

"Not to worry," she told him, "I'll catch her at lunchtime and get the details."

He looked ridiculously relieved.

* * *

"This is the second one?" Mike Parton asked as Callie showed him the scene.

He stood well back from the body of the old lady as he spoke, not yet sure if this was a crime scene. Dressed in his usual dark grey suit, white shirt and black tie, and with an air of quiet dignity, he looked like a funeral director. To be fair, that wasn't far from the truth: a retired policeman who now worked for the coroner, Parton dealt with death on a daily basis. In cases of sudden and unexpected death, Parton and Callie, the local forensic physician, needed to decide if it was due to natural causes in which case it would simply require a post-mortem and inquest; or if there was any possibility of it being due to anything unnatural: negligence, suicide, accident or even murder, in which cases it would require police attendance and a forensic team.

"That's right," she answered pulling out her notebook to check the information she had got from Caroline Stratton after Angus had left. "The first was a Mr Alan Darling, lived up in Ore."

Parton frowned.

"I don't remember the name."

"No, well, I don't think you were called," she explained. "He was eighty-eight, with congestive heart failure, COPD, and poorly-controlled type 2 diabetes, so the GP was happy to certify death and it wasn't a coroner's case."

He nodded that he agreed with that course of action.

"However, the doctor involved mentioned it as being strange that he was all dressed up, ready to go out and it stuck in Dr McPhail's mind."

"So, he called you and passed the buck," Parton said with a smile.

Which was exactly what Angus had done, Callie had to agree.

"I can't see any signs of carbon monoxide poisoning, there's no note or evidence of it being suicide." Callie paused and looked round. "It's almost certainly a natural death and Billy will find a massive coronary occlusion, but—"

"Yes," Parton agreed. "There is a 'but', isn't there? It's all definitely a bit odd." He thought for a moment before turning to Callie, suddenly decisive. "Right, let's get this show on the road."

* * *

When Callie returned to the small, ancient, terraced cottage after her afternoon surgery, she could see that Parton had been right to call it a show – even though she had probably missed the main part, as the lack of the mortuary van suggested that the body had been removed. A crime scene vehicle was parked on double yellow lines just down the street from the house where the road was a bit wider. There was tape across the pavement in front of the house, causing pedestrians to walk into the road to get by, with most of them peering into the open front door as they did so. Callie hoped they'd be able to take the tape down soon before someone got run over.

She was pleased to see that there was no longer a policeman standing guard, noting the details of everyone who entered the house, and that from the look of it, the forensic team were finished and packing up. Well, Callie noticed, the last remaining member of the forensic team was packing up. Everyone else had already been and gone, leaving their colleague to finish up. Neighbours were still watching from the comfort of their own homes, but there were few rubberneckers, probably due to the slight but constant drizzle and the fact that the only safe place to stand and watch was the churchyard opposite and there was no shelter there. A sunny day and it would have been packed. Callie also hoped that the rain had kept the press at bay.

"Excuse me?" a voice asked, and Callie turned to see an elderly lady standing by the entrance to the churchyard.

"Can I help?" As Callie approached the woman, she could see that she wasn't as old as she had appeared at first sight. It was her clothes and her general demeanour that made her seem old.

"Is Mrs Mount all right?" the woman asked.

"Can I ask who you are?"

"Jean Lovejoy," the woman answered. "I live round the corner and visit Mrs Mount, do her bits of shopping, stuff like that."

"I'm sorry to say that Mrs Mount has died," Callie said gently, "but I'm sure that she was very grateful for all your help."

"Oh dear" – the woman seemed sad rather than shocked – "I suppose it was to be expected, given her age." Her gaze shifted to a white-suited figure that had just emerged from the house. "Was it a murder, then?"

"Just unexpected," Callie explained. She didn't want to start any rumours. "We have to be cautious when we don't know exactly what happened. Excuse me." Callie turned and hurried across to the CSI who was carrying a number of evidence bags out of the front door. "Hi, how's it going?"

The CSI pulled down her mask, but continued walking towards the van as she replied.

"Nearly done here, Dr Hughes. The body's gone to the mortuary. Do you want a quick look round before I secure the premises?"

"Yes, please."

Callie went to the house, leaving the CSI busy logging all the evidence and placing it in the containers in the back of the van. Although the precaution was probably unnecessary as the forensic team had finished with the scene, and despite having been in the house once already, Callie suited up before entering. It was always best to be careful; there was always the chance that a scene would have to be re-examined in the light of new information. Callie knew that leaving her prints, hairs or other bits of detritus at a crime scene was best avoided if at all possible.

The house seemed less eerie now that the body had gone, more ordinary. The low-ceilinged living room was clean and polished and as full of ornaments, artificial flowers and lacy mats as she remembered, but now that she had time to look more closely, she could see that there were no photographs of loved ones, which was sad. The chair the body had been sitting in was placed cosily next to the inglenook fireplace, but there was no sign of a fire having been set any time recently. Just as well, Callie thought; open fires and old people with dementia were not a good mix.

The tiny kitchen had an old-fashioned cooker with an eye-level grill, a sink and an empty draining board. No dishwasher – there really wasn't enough room. Callie opened the fridge with her gloved hands. It was empty. Not even the remains of a pint of milk, some limp lettuce or the overripe tomato that her own fridge always seemed to have in it.

A brief check of the kitchen bin, completely empty with not even a rubbish bag to line it, told Callie that Mrs Mount had sincerely believed she was going away on holiday and cleared everything out in preparation. She didn't want to come back to a smelly bin or mouldy cheese.

Callie went up the stairs. The nurse had been right, they were very steep and an absolute death-trap despite the handrail and an extra rope to hang on to. At the top she found a tiny bathroom, with a wickedly uneven floor, and a small, neat bedroom – bed made and covered with a faded yellow candlewick bedspread.

The bedside table was clear, but at last Callie found a photograph. It was of a wedding, and from the style of clothes Callie thought that it must have taken place in the 1960s. Lifting up the picture to get a better look, Callie thought she recognised where it had been taken: not the church opposite, but outside St Clements Church in All Saints Street. The couple in the picture were young and smiling and happy. The bride was in white with a short veil, and was just about recognisable as a younger version of the woman whose body had been in the chair downstairs. Callie wondered what had happened to the man, her husband. There were no men's clothes in the wardrobe and no razor in the bathroom. The fact that the photograph was still by her bed suggested the man had left through death rather than divorce. She would check with Angus later.

There were no other photos, no pictures of children and grandchildren growing up, leading Callie to suspect that there were unlikely to be any next of kin. Callie took a longer look at the wedding picture, thinking about the hopes the bride must have had on such a happy day and wondering what had gone wrong.

"Dr Hughes?"

Callie was startled out of her reverie by the CSI calling up the stairs.

"Coming!" she called back. "I'm all done." She headed down the stairs so that the CSI could secure the premises and leave.

* * *

"No, but it was really weird," Callie was telling her boyfriend, Billy Iqbal, that evening as they ate in their favourite haunt, Porters Wine Bar. He smiled and took a sip of his lager.

"In what way?"

"She was sitting there, all ready to go on holiday, just waiting for her taxi to arrive."

"But she was dead."

"Exactly."

"Well, I didn't have time to do anything by the time she got to me," Billy told her. "But I promise I'll take a closer look first thing in the morning." He thought for a moment. "Although I won't be able to do the PM until the afternoon. Got a management meeting." He grimaced at the thought, and then brightened. "If your visit list isn't too awful, you could come and watch."

Callie thought about that. She would like to be there, but it really did depend on how busy things were at the surgery.

"I'll see what I can do."

They paused their conversation whilst the waitress brought their food over. They had learnt that discussing some things in front of an audience was unwise. Postmortems and bizarre deaths being among them.

Billy was currently the pathologist in charge of the mortuary at the local hospital, but ambition meant that he would be leaving soon to take up a post in Northern Ireland. Whilst Callie fully understood that it had become increasingly frustrating for him to watch his most interesting cases being taken over by Home Office pathologists even though he had passed all the qualifications, the thought of him leaving made her sad. Much as she wanted to try, she wasn't sure they would be able to sustain a long-distance relationship. She had thought about going with him, but they didn't live together in Hastings, both preferring to maintain a degree of independence. Her head told her that if she wasn't certain their relationship would survive seeing less of each other, it would be madness to give up her own career, home, friends and family to follow him in the hope that it worked out.

That didn't stop her from being angry that the only vacancy was so far away and wasn't even a Home Office post as Belfast came under the Northern Ireland Office. Billy was taking the job in the hope that once a vacancy came up in a group practice in England, and with some experience under his belt, he would be able to return. It was just a shame the move was coming so early in their relationship. Given more time, the relationship might just have developed into something stronger.

Once the waitress had left Callie looked at her chicken salad and sighed. It looked lovely but, as always, she now wished she had chosen what Billy had. The Goan fish curry looked and smelled amazing.

It was so unfair. There was no denying that Billy looked good too. Thirty-nine years old and the only signs of ageing were laughter lines at the corners of his dark brown, almond shaped eyes. Despite eating out regularly, having takeaways and Billy cooking some fabulous meals for them both, he never seemed to put on weight. Callie, however, had noticed that some of her clothes were getting a little bit tight, so she was doing her best to stop the rot. There was no doubt that there were fewer calories in her salad, but she wouldn't enjoy it as much and a little bit of her said that she would have plenty of time to diet once he had left. So long as she didn't comfort eat. She took a sip of her Pinot Grigio – she was going to have to watch she didn't comfort drink as well.

"It's a shame the first patient wasn't autopsied," Billy continued.

"Yes, but understandable. His death wasn't unexpected."

"Will his GP be agreeable to talking to me? Giving me his history and such like, do you think?"

"I reckon so. She's married to Angus, the doctor who called me because he felt there was something wrong."

She didn't add that Angus was a ditherer and his wife had little patience with him. Right now, she could picture them in their enormous and comfortable farmhouse kitchen where Caroline would be telling her husband he was making a fuss about nothing. Callie hoped she didn't say the same to Billy because, much as one body could be written off as nothing sinister, two smacked of something more, and three? If there were ever another one, well, that would definitely lead her to suspect murder.

# Chapter 3

Callie sat at her desk and viewed her consultation list with a sigh. It was long. People often asked her why she didn't choose one career over the other, be a full-time police doctor or a full-time GP instead of trying to juggle the two. The truth was that she had periods of boredom with both jobs and at least the variety was increased by doing both. Like all work, most of it was mundane. Coughs and colds as a GP and drink and drugs as a police doctor, but then a really interesting case would come along: a patient whose illness was out of the ordinary, where she could really help, or a sudden death that might be suspicious, such as the one she had attended the day before.

Callie knew a lot of what drove her was curiosity, and that, try as she might, if she didn't go to the post-mortem on Mrs Mount, she would find it hard not to wonder what Billy was discovering. She would have to move some of her visits, but she was sure she could fit at least one in before evening surgery if it was urgent, and the rest would have to be done after. A late night, but the surgery staff, and her patients, were all used to it. She picked up the phone; the important thing was to stop more visits being added during the morning.

"Hi, Linda." Callie heard the practice manager sigh as she realised what Callie was about to ask her to do.

Callie always felt guilty letting her colleagues down and making them do more than their fair share so that she could pursue her other work, but then, she reminded herself, that was why she wasn't a partner. They only paid her for part-time work, and she always worked more than her allotted hours anyway, so there was no reason to feel guilty. Having given herself a mental talking-to, she tucked a stray strand of her straight blonde hair behind her ear and pressed the buzzer for the first patient of the day.

\* \* \*

It wasn't until about halfway through her morning surgery that Monica Claydon came in, or rather shuffled in. Everything about her – her movements, her stance, her face – suggested extreme weariness. She was formally dressed for the office where she worked, but Callie noticed that her blouse was slightly creased, definitely a sign that all was not well with this normally meticulously neat and dignified black woman. Callie also remembered her as being vigorous and energetic, but she certainly wasn't either of those things at the moment.

"Have a seat, Monica," Callie told her patient, as she glanced at the screen in front of her.

Monica seemed to have seen every doctor in the practice over the last few months. Always complaining of similar problems: tiredness, aching joints, intermittent fevers, a lack of appetite; the list of non-specific symptoms went on and on. The problem facing all the doctors was that so many illnesses had TATT, or tiredness all the time, as their main symptom, that it was often difficult to tie down the exact cause in each case.

"How can I help you?" Callie asked once Monica was settled in a chair.

"I don't know," Monica replied in a voice that spoke of despair. "I'm not sure anyone can, but something is wrong with me, that's for sure."

"Can you tell me how you feel?" Callie asked.

"The same as I have every other time I've been in," Monica replied. "Can't you just read what it says?" Callie could see that Monica wasn't being stroppy; she just didn't seem to have enough energy to go over her symptoms again.

Callie looked at the notes her colleagues had put in Monica's record. She had presented with a swollen right knee and had been prescribed anti-inflammatories and painkillers. They didn't seem to have helped. One doctor had also prescribed antidepressants, arguing that she was probably depressed, although he didn't know whether the depression was causing the symptoms or vice versa.

Next, Callie checked what tests had been done. These were primarily blood tests; she went through the results of all of them, and there were a lot. Her colleagues had been very thorough. Monica's ESR was raised, suggesting some sort of inflammatory process, and her liver enzymes were mildly abnormal. The rheumatoid factor was not raised, and neither were her uric acid or creatinine levels, suggesting that rheumatoid arthritis and gout were unlikely. Her full blood count was normal and there was no sign of sickle cell disease. Nothing else had been found.

All in all, everything she would have done had already been done by her colleagues.

"And there's nothing new?" Callie queried.

"No. Nothing's changed. No better, no worse."

"Do the tablets work?"

"The painkillers help the pain, but they don't make me feel better. The happy pills don't seem to do much at all."

Callie smiled at the reference to the antidepressants as "happy pills", but it was a shame they didn't seem to have helped.

"You should persevere with them anyway," she told Monica. "Can you pop up on the couch so that I can examine you?" Callie stood and indicated her examination table, beginning to pull the curtains round.

"I don't know if I can pop anywhere," Monica said with a hint of her old humour as she pulled herself up from her chair with difficulty. "My poppin' days are long gone."

Callie smiled.

"Well, if you can remove any outer clothing down to your undies and then get up onto the couch, there's a paper sheet you can use to cover yourself. If you can't manage, give a shout and I'll help."

Callie closed the curtain and took a closer look at all the notes from her colleagues who had examined Monica in the past. There really didn't seem to be anything that stood out to give her a clue as to what the cause of her symptoms could be.

"Are you ready for me?" Callie asked once she heard Monica settle.

"Yes, doctor."

Callie opened the curtains, pulling on a pair of gloves.

"Now tell me if anything I do hurts," she said as she started to examine the patient. She started at the head, pulling down Monica's eyelids to look for signs of anaemia, even though she knew from the blood tests that her haemoglobin levels were fine. Then she worked her way down Monica's body, feeling for lumps and bumps. In the neck, under the arms, the groin, anywhere that glands might be enlarged in an infection. Whilst she felt very slightly shotty or gritty glands in some areas, there were no definite signs to tell her what was going on. Callie ran her hands over Monica's skin. It was hard to see rashes when the skin was as dark as Monica's, so Callie was trying to feel for any roughness, bumps or heat that might tell her a rash was present. Nothing. Although Monica grimaced when any of her limbs were moved or prodded by Callie, it was her left knee that was most sore, and it was definitely swollen and felt hot to the touch.

"Right," Callie said as she took off her gloves. "You can get dressed now."

When Monica re-emerged from behind the curtains, fully dressed again, Callie was already printing off a blood test request form.

"More blood tests, I'm afraid. That one's a more detailed look at your blood cells and these are looking for other inflammatory diseases." Callie showed Monica what she meant on the form. "And I think we should refer you to a rheumatologist, if that's all right? See if he can help us with a diagnosis."

"I thought the other doctor said that I didn't have rheumatism?"

"Your test was negative but, as you said, something is definitely going on, and I think a rheumatologist is the best person to advise us about where to go from here, okay?"

Monica nodded in agreement.

"Whatever you say, doctor, I just want to feel well again."

"I know. Oh, and I've changed your painkiller, to see if that works any better."

She handed her patient the form and new prescription and watched her leave, hoping that, at the very least, the referral would generate a plan of action that would actually help the patient, because just managing the pain clearly wasn't the answer.

* * *

Callie often visited the local mortuary, partly because of her work as a forensic physician, but more because of a desire to see Billy, and to have a decent cup of coffee. He had a state-of-the-art coffee machine in his office that was certainly a step up from the instant she would get in the surgery unless she surreptitiously raided the senior partners' personal coffee store. She would have bought herself a coffee machine for her consulting room, but even in their new, larger premises, there really wasn't enough room for one.

In truth, there wasn't really room for a coffee machine in Billy's office, but he had made the space by putting the printer on the floor where he had to step over it to sit at his desk. It was a question of priorities. That, and the fact that he didn't have patients coming into his office where it would have been a potential trip hazard. Being a pathologist had its benefits.

As she sat, waiting for him to get back from his meeting, Callie gave some thought to their relationship.

She liked Billy. He wasn't her best friend, because Kate was that, but he was a close second. She liked spending time with him, he made her laugh, he could cook and the sex was great. But did she love him? She thought the answer was yes, but how could she be sure? How could she be sure enough to give up everything she had in Hastings and move to Northern Ireland?

"Hiya, just finished." Billy breezed into the room and lit it up with his big smile and sunny personality, making Callie wonder why she was so hesitant. Maybe she should go away with him. Maybe he was the one.

\* \* \*

Callie looked closely at the body laid out in front of them as Billy, voice slightly muffled by a mask and visor, spoke into a microphone hanging down from the ceiling. Billy liked a belt-and-braces approach to making sure everything was recorded so that he had all the information he needed to write his report. Jim, the mortuary technician, was assisting at the post-mortem and was making notes as well; he would also photograph anything of interest that the pathologist pointed out.

"Body of a well-nourished female, known to be aged eighty-two and the visual examination fits with that."

Once he had completed his overall visual check, Billy began moving down the body, moving the head from side to side, feeling the neck, checking for any enlarged lymph nodes there, and then in the supraclavicular fossa and armpits, but finding nothing. So far, it was a very similar examination to the one Callie had given Monica the day before.

Billy lifted Mrs Mount's right arm, checking it all the way down to her hands. He inspected both aspects of her hand. There was no sign of injury, or any dirt under the nails. Of course, if it was decided that any crime had been committed, underneath the fingernails would be scraped so that anything, however microscopic, could be examined.

Billy leant across and did the same on the left arm.

"Evidence of recent bruising in the left cubital fossa." Billy was looking at the inside of Mrs Mount's left elbow and indicated for his assistant to photograph it. From where Callie was standing, she could see there was quite a bruise.

"It looks like she had blood taken recently," she commented.

"Hmm." Billy got closer and examined the bruising. "There's certainly a hypodermic mark there, and it's quite big, almost like she flinched and the needle tore the skin." He spent some more time closely examining the area before moving on.

The rest of the post-mortem, both external and internal, revealed nothing abnormal. Mrs Mount had been in good health generally, just as Angus had maintained. Yes, she was old, and yes, she probably got confused due to her dementia, but there was nothing else to explain why she had died so suddenly. It was down to the coroner to decide if any further action was needed, but Callie knew it was unlikely unless there was something abnormal found in the bloods and other samples that Billy had taken and sent off for further analysis. Old ladies of eighty-two died, sometimes simply because their bodies were just too tired to carry on. There was certainly no evidence of foul play or any reason for her, or the police, to be involved, so far.

# Chapter 4

Saturday morning brunch with her best friend, Kate, a local solicitor, was a ritual Callie would be sad to lose if she left the town and moved to Northern Ireland to be with Billy. True, it was sometimes moved to a Sunday if Callie was working, or Kate didn't want to leave her bed or the man of the moment, but a weekend never went by without them meeting up; they quite often went for a girls' night out in the week as well, if their jobs didn't get in the way. Kate was Callie's sounding board when she worked through problems in both her work and home life. They had been friends through thick and thin, with Kate saving her life many times metaphorically and once in reality, when she was able to alert the police and tell them that Callie had been abducted.

As they sat in their usual seats in the café, savouring their wildly differing tastes in breakfast and breathing in the warm steam from Kate's cappuccino and Callie's tea, while watching the tourists ambling up and down the High Street, it was hard to imagine ever leaving.

"Do you think it was the excitement of going away that killed them?" Kate asked. They had been discussing the deaths of the two elderly people, and how nothing unnatural seemed to have caused them.

"No idea." Callie shrugged. "It's possible, I suppose."

"In some ways, it's nice, isn't it?"

Callie raised her eyebrow in question.

"That when they died, they were looking forward to something enjoyable. A happy event."

"I suppose so." Callie gave this idea some thought. "You're right. It is nice. They both lived alone from what I heard, no family around to help, and neither of them were well off. The lady whose house I went to, well, it looked like she was living quite a meagre existence, you know?"

Kate nodded and wiped the last bit of toast around her plate, to soak up the remaining egg yolk, bacon fat and tomato sauce that was there.

"Do you know where either of them was going?" she asked before popping the toast in her mouth.

"No," Callie admitted and then thought about that as well. "Where do elderly people, especially those who are perhaps a little confused, go on holiday, do you think?" she asked. "Is there a travel company that specialises in that sort of clientele?"

"Dunno. SAGA? Confused.com?" Kate grinned. "Do you think they come back with the same number they start off with, or do they lose a few on the way?"

"Stop it!" Callie couldn't help laughing at the idea. "That's awful."

But the more she thought about it, the more she wondered. Did a charity run holidays for elderly and mildly confused patients? If so, she had quite a few patients who might be interested in it. She would just have to make sure they didn't get overexcited about going away and die – that would never do.

* * *

Callie spent most of the rest of her weekend with Billy, enjoying his company. Not wanting to put a dampener on their time together, they both avoided the subject of his impending departure. The time was going to come, and come soon, when they couldn't ignore it any longer and would have to sit down and discuss their future, together or apart. The fact that neither had spoken of it yet, not to mention that Callie had made no plans to leave her job or her home, probably said more than mere words ever could.

It wasn't until Monday lunchtime, when she was sitting in the doctor's shared office, dealing with a pile of prescription requests, going through test results, that Callie heard any more about Mrs Mount when Billy called.

"Do you know this Angus McPhail bloke?" he asked her.

"I've met him, yes," was Callie's cautious reply.

She could well understand Billy's irritation if Angus had been his usual self, generally dithering and lacking the confidence to give anything like a straight reply to a question.

"I can't deal with him," Billy told her, bluntly. "Getting a straight answer out of the guy is just impossible. His wife, in contrast, was completely on the ball and gave me all the information I needed about her patient" – there was a moment's hesitation whilst he checked his notes – "Alan Darling. She was a great help, although there's not much to suggest anything other than natural causes in his case."

"What did you want to know from Angus?" Callie asked cautiously. Goodness only knew she didn't want to get involved with him, but if needs must, she would do so.

"What blood tests Mrs Mount had had recently, but he said he couldn't find any on the system." He paused. "At least, I think that's what he meant, he didn't really seem sure. He ummed and aahed and kept saying he'd check somewhere else, looking in different places, in case he'd missed it or something. He actually told me someone might have asked for a test verbally, I mean, does that even happen?"

"Not usually." Callie thought about how it might. "If I want a blood test done, I have to print out a form for the patient to take, or I would email it to them. If the phlebotomist or the community nurse were going to take the blood, I'd email it to their office and I would tell them I was doing it, to make sure it didn't get missed."

"But you wouldn't just tell them to do the test?"

"No. You can't send a sample to the lab without a form, so even if you did ask the nurse to do it, or took it yourself, you would still need to generate a form so the lab can send back the result and that form would be in the records."

Callie could remember the days when test request forms were all filled out by hand, as were prescriptions, and she would have a stack of different types of forms on her desk. It was possible and even common for a doctor to forget to write in the notes what tests or drugs they had ordered for a patient and it led to all manner of mix-ups if a patient saw someone else, but nowadays, everything was on the computer system, and everything was recorded in the patient's electronic notes. That way, there were far fewer mistakes.

In theory, anyway.

If Angus or one of his partners had asked for a blood test, it should be on the system, whether he could find it or not.

However, if she had been seen at the hospital, it might not be.

"Can you check her hospital notes and see if she was seen by anyone there? They might have ordered a test."

"Of course, and I can check with the lab as well, see if they have a record of anything there." Billy sounded relieved to have a way forward that didn't mean speaking to Angus again.

"I'll get the practice manager at Angus's surgery to check Mrs Mount's records. She'll be able to find her way round and tell us if any tests were ordered, even if Angus can't."

* * *

The practice manager at the surgery where Angus McPhail worked was able to tell Callie that no blood tests had been ordered for Mrs Mount in the last three months and the results of those most recent ones had been received a week later, so the bruising on her arm could not be for a surgery-requested test. She also told Callie that Mrs Mount had not been referred to the hospital. All in all, she was at a loss to explain why the patient had had a blood test done.

"She's too old to have given blood or anything."

It seemed odd to Callie too, and when she left a message on Billy's answerphone letting him know the outcome of her enquiries, she said so.

"Is it possible she was given some kind of intravenous infusion?" she queried, knowing as she did so that this was unlikely.

IVs were more likely to be given elsewhere, in the veins of the lower arm or back of the hand, but she couldn't think of any other reason for the injury. She hoped he was having more luck finding out what might have happened at the hospital.

"Maybe she was seen in A&E or something?"

While electronic records meant far less delay in the transfer of data regarding patients seen at the hospital, Callie knew from her own experience that things often went awry. She just hoped Billy was able to track down exactly where Mrs Mount had been treated.

# Chapter 5

Callie was on her fifth visit of the afternoon and was feeling tired, irritated and damp. The rain seemed to stop the moment she got inside the houses and start again whenever she got out. She had an umbrella with her, as she always did, but constantly getting in and out of the car was impossible without getting a little bit wet. She would have been better off walking between visits, with her umbrella up all the way, had they been less widely spread out. What was worse, she couldn't park on the driveway of the last house she was supposed to be visiting, because of a blue Nissan Micra parked there.

As she reached the front porch of the semi-detached house, she lowered her umbrella and shook out the worst of the water, before ringing the doorbell.

To Callie's surprise the door was opened by the community nurse whose name Callie still couldn't remember.

"Hello, Dr Hughes. Mrs Stanhope didn't say you were coming today."

The nurse seemed cross that she had come and Callie wasn't quite sure how she was expected to respond to this comment.

"She's on my visit list. I wanted to check her cellulitis."

"I've just finished dressing her legs."

That explained her belligerence, she didn't want Callie messing up her work.

"That's fine, um," Callie struggled with the name, and the nurse still wasn't wearing her name badge. "I'm sure I can take a look without disturbing the dressings."

The nurse didn't look as if she had any confidence that Callie would be able to do that and she hesitated.

"It's okay, you don't have to stay, honestly. I can redress the legs if I need to," Callie reassured her.

The nurse harrumphed and still hesitated but a quick look at her watch seemed to help her make a decision.

"Okay, I've got other things to do," she said, pushing past Callie and hurrying to her car, holding a file of patient notes over her head to keep herself dry. She clearly wasn't worried about the paperwork getting wet.

Callie stepped into the hallway and closed the door behind her.

"She's a right sourpuss, that one," Mrs Stanhope said with a smile as Callie came into the brightly lit and over-heated sitting room. Callie was pleased to see her with her legs raised on a footstool.

"She is, isn't she?" Callie agreed. "I can never remember her name, either."

"Not sure I know it," Mrs Stanhope said. "Can't say that she ever really introduced herself."

Callie picked up the folder that was kept in the patient's home so that everyone could write in what they had done. Despite most of the medical professionals who did home visits having electronic devices to update patient records remotely, the red folder remained a vital source of information.

The nurse had written in there that Mrs Stanhope had had her dressing done, but her signature was indecipherable, so there was no help from that quarter.

"How's your cellulitis doing?" Callie asked her patient, pointing to her legs.

"Much the same," the patient answered. "Those pills you gave me don't seem to be doing any good."

\* \* \*

"Her bloods came back," Billy said when Callie kissed him as he stirred more paprika into the chicken stroganoff he was making for their dinner. It smelled amazing. There would be definite plus points to moving in with him, she thought, and that idea and the fact that she had just come in from work meant it took her a moment or two to realise that he was referring to Mrs Mount.

"Normal?" she queried, hanging up her coat and kicking off her shoes.

The stroganoff might well be delicious but having just seen the amount of cream he had added, Callie was planning on not eating too much of it. Planning being the operative word. What was it Oscar Wilde had said about being able to resist everything but temptation? Her willpower seemed to have gone to pot recently.

"No." Billy lifted the spoon to his mouth and tasted the sauce. "Perfect." Having given his opinion of the sauce he went back to stirring. "Her potassium was high."

"It always goes up after death, doesn't it?"

"Yes, but her level was really high, plus, it was higher in the cardiac blood than the general circulation or the vitreous fluid, although that can sometimes take longer to go up."

Callie knew that pathologists often measured the levels of potassium in the vitreous humour, the gel-like fluid found in the eye, as its more linear rate of increase after death than in the blood could give an indication of time of death, although it still wasn't the absolute indication that the police, and crime fiction aficionados, always wanted. The levels of potassium went up in the general circulation after death, but if the cardiac blood level was higher, that might indicate it as a cause of death.

"High enough to ring alarm bells?"

"Possibly, or possibly not. It was sort of on the cusp, but her blood chloride levels were up too."

"Oh?" Callie sat up. That was much more interesting. "You think she had ingested salt just before she died? Did you find much in her stomach contents?"

"No, very little."

"What about her sodium levels?"

"Normal."

There was a moment or two of silence as Callie thought about that.

"So—"

"I think it's possible that she could have been given an infusion, or bolus injection, of potassium chloride."

There was a lot of ambiguity in that statement rather than definite evidence, but both Callie and Billy knew what it meant if she had been given it. Potassium chloride used to be added to drips in some instances but because it could disrupt heart activity if too strong a solution was used, or it wasn't mixed properly, it was now rarely prescribed except in pre-mixed dilute solutions. It was still used in a concentrated form in some countries where lethal injections were used for executions, along with other drugs which would paralyse and sedate the patient while the potassium chloride stopped the heart.

"And no, there was no trace of barbiturates or pancuronium bromide in her blood, like they use in lethal injections," he added, having clearly been thinking along the same lines.

Callie thought about that. Using just potassium chloride would work, but she suspected it would have been a painful way to die. A very painful way. She shivered.

"Have your referred it on?"

Billy sighed. Callie knew it was a big call to make.

"I went back and sent samples from the bruised tissue around the site, in the hope they would be conclusive, but they weren't."

"But that only tells you that all the drug went into the blood stream and the bruising occurred as she moved in response."

"I know." He sighed again. "So I did all the paperwork and then spoke to Mike Parton before pressing send. He told me to sleep on it, but he'd support my decision either way."

Callie didn't think the stroganoff was benefitting from the vigorous stirring it was getting, but Billy didn't seem to notice.

"As I will. You know that."

Billy gave her a long hard look.

"You think there's something wrong about the death, don't you?"

"Well, yes. The way she was found, the other man, I can't believe it's natural."

Billy stopped stirring and picked up his phone. After a couple of button presses and some scrolling, his thumb hovered for a moment, before there was a decisive tap.

"There."

"You've sent it?" Callie couldn't stop the slight quiver in her voice.

"No point in sleeping on it," Billy told her with a small, anxious smile. "I wouldn't have slept anyway."

Callie didn't think he would even now.

"So," Billy continued, "Mike Parton will organise another PM as soon as possible and he was going to see Steve Miller in CID in any event, to warn them about the possible need to get an investigation up and running."

Billy seemed relieved to have made the decision and started serving their dinner, but suddenly Callie didn't feel quite so hungry.

# Chapter 6

Callie called into the police station before going to work the next day. She knew Miller would want to talk to her as she had been present at the scene and had been the one to call out the coroner's officer, if only because Angus was dithering. She had decided that she would save Miller the trouble of trying to get hold of her later in the day and the disruption that would inevitably cause to her surgery list. She was only given ten minutes to see each patient, so stopping to speak to someone for even a relatively short while would upset quite a number of them. Not to mention the practice manager.

With some uncertainty still as to whether or not this was a crime, the main CID office hadn't been turned into a full-blown incident room as yet. Callie knew that once a major investigation was running, all those not involved in it were moved out into smaller offices scattered around the building so that there were no distractions from the main event. However, in this instance, while everything possible would be done to make sure that no evidence was lost, there was still the chance that the Home Office pathologist would disagree with Billy and decide the levels of potassium and chloride were roughly within normal limits.

That would make Mrs Mount's death due to natural causes and the investigation would be stopped before it had ever really started. She could understand Miller thinking that there was no point in doing major reorganisations just yet.

Callie didn't think the Home Office pathologist would disagree with Billy though – at least, she hoped not. He needed to have been very sure that something was wrong before calling it suspicious. Billy knew a false move at this stage would follow him around in his chosen career and possibly ruin it before he had even started. He had thought long and hard before coming to the decision that he had to voice his concerns: missing a suspicious death would be even worse than raising the alarm unnecessarily.

As she went into the large, open-plan office, Callie braced herself to be met by a rude comment from Detective Sergeant Bob Jeffries, a man guaranteed to rub even the most tolerant person up the wrong way. She was relieved not to see him lurking anywhere in the room and smiled and waved at some of the faces she recognised. DS Jayne Hales, who Callie considered a friend as well as a colleague, and DC Nigel Nugent, who always got given the technical work with regard to computers or phones as he was the only one on the team who really understood them. She could see Detective Inspector Steve Miller through the windows of the small office that was, in reality, nothing more than a partitioned-off section of the larger room with windows on each side enabling him to see what was going on. Given that the walls were just plasterboard, he could pretty much hear everything that was going on, too. The illusion of privacy was nothing more than that – an illusion.

Callie quickly made her way across to the office and gave a gentle knock before opening the door.

Miller looked up as she entered his office and, once he'd registered who it was standing there, smiled. It was a very nice smile, but that was no excuse for the slight flip of Callie's stomach in response. It was true that DI Miller was a ruggedly good-looking man in his late thirties, with a few strands of grey adding distinction to his brown hair. There were laughter lines by his hazel eyes, and his smile, rare though it was when he was at work, could melt the hardest of hearts. But all that was no excuse, Callie told herself firmly. She was, after all, in love with Billy.

"Good morning," she said brightly as she came in and closed the door behind her, hoping that they wouldn't be disturbed. She knew it was going to be hard enough to convince him that someone had killed one elderly person in the town, let alone two. "I have a late start this morning so I thought I'd come in and talk to you about Mrs Mount."

"Great," Miller replied. "Have a seat. Can I get you a coffee? Or tea?"

He half rose before Callie waved the offer away.

"I'm fine, thanks." She'd tasted what passed for tea and coffee in the incident room before. "Right, what do you need to know?" she said once she was seated and sure that she had Miller's full attention.

"You tell me," was his very unhelpful reply. Suddenly, he saw something in the main room and he stood up and opened his office door. "Bob!" He called to DS Jeffries, who had just come into the main office.

Callie realised he must have just nipped out to the lavatory, because his instinctive reaction was to check his flies were safely done up before hurrying towards his boss's office.

Miller turned back to Callie.

"He's going to want to hear this," he said by way of explanation.

Callie's heart sank. Bob Jeffries might well want to hear it, but she wasn't sure she wanted to tell him, and she certainly didn't want to hear his thoughts on the case, if there was a case at all. Her optimism at entering the office plummeted and she might have said something except that she thought she detected a slight twinkle in Miller's eye, suggesting that he was deliberately winding her up by inviting Jeffries in. If that was his game, she wasn't going to rise to it, that was for sure.

Jeffries came into the office and lounged against a filing cabinet. Callie was glad he hadn't offered her a hand to shake, as she suspected he probably wouldn't have washed them after his trip to the toilet, despite government advice that he should do so. The thought of him standing at a sink singing "Happy Birthday" as he washed made her smile. There was zero chance of him doing that.

While Miller was always smart and clean cut, smelling lightly of sandalwood and soap, Jeffries always managed to look scruffy and usually had bits of food stuck to his shirt or tie.

"Do you really think a crime has been committed?" Miller asked her.

"Dr Iqbal thinks so, and he is a very good pathologist." Callie was immediately on the defensive. "And I have to agree that there is something a bit suspicious about the two deaths."

"Two?" Miller sat forward, suddenly interested and she even had Jeffries' attention.

"Thought it was just the one old dear," he said.

"Two. Mrs Mount and a Mr Alan Darling."

Miller hastily looked at his computer and checked through a report.

"There's nothing here about an Alan Darling," he said finally and looked accusingly at her.

"No, well, he was put down as a natural death – not a coroner's case."

"So why are you including him now?"

"Because he was found in similar circumstances."

"High blood levels of this" – Miller checked what was on his screen again – "potassium and er, chloride?"

"Well, we don't know because he didn't have a post-mortem and–"

"So why are you including him?"

37

"Because he was found sitting in his chair, suitcase packed, all ready to go on holiday, just like Mrs Mount."

"But his doctor didn't think it was suspicious?"

"Well, no. He was quite sick, so his death wasn't completely unexpected."

"So, if his doctor wasn't suspicious and the coroner wasn't alerted, and no PM or tests were done—"

"He's dead and buried, so to speak." This was from Jeffries, of course.

"Cremated," Callie admitted. "He's been cremated."

"So, there's nothing we can do," Jeffries added, unnecessarily in Callie's view. She glared at him. Miller cleared his throat, aware that what he was about to say wasn't what she wanted to hear.

"I think we have to leave that one out. We don't even have a body to exhume, after all." Not that he'd want to exhume a body unless he absolutely had to. It was always difficult with relatives and the press, Callie knew, and was definitely a last resort.

"Yes, but it—"

"Let's just concentrate on Mrs Mount for now," he said firmly.

"All right," Callie said with a sigh. "But I reserve the right to bring him up again later."

"Thought you said he'd been cremated." Jeffries smirked.

Callie glared at him, and having made her point, she settled to tell them about the woman she had seen.

"Mrs Mount was found sitting in her chair, as if waiting to go on holiday, just like Mr Darling." She couldn't help herself, she really couldn't. Even if it did earn her a stern look from Miller. "There was bruising in her left cubital fossa, here" — she indicated the inner aspect of her elbow — "suggesting she had had blood taken recently, but no record of that blood being taken, or requested at either her doctor's surgery or the hospital." Callie was glad that Billy had checked records and been able to tell her, with some degree of certainty, that there hadn't had been samples taken there.

"How can you be sure no one took blood?" Jeffries said. "Or gave her an injection for that matter? From what I hear, the NHS can't even get the right patient much of the time, let alone find their past notes."

"It's easier now with the computer systems. It's all there on the screen, no bits of paper to get lost." Callie mentally crossed her fingers that she wasn't proven wrong in this case. She could cite half a dozen instances of missing test results and incomplete electronic notes from memory, let alone problems with different systems talking to each other. And that was only in the last couple of months, but she wasn't about to tell DS Jeffries that.

"But there's no doubt that someone needs to make enquiries. Be absolutely sure about what's happened," she said firmly.

"But it might still be a natural death."

"Yes, but—"

"And forensics have already been over the scene and collected evidence, so we can wait until we hear from the Home Office pathologist, before doing anything more."

Callie sighed. She knew Miller was trying to be as reasonable as possible, and she really couldn't ask for anything more.

# Chapter 7

It was Callie's morning for catching up with administration. She was busy in the shared office at the top of the surgery building, checking test results, approving prescription requests and dealing with letters to and from hospital consultants. While it meant a period of comparative peace and quiet, and some doctors really liked the time it gave them away from seeing the sick or worried-well, Callie found it quite tedious. She loved the face-to-face contact with patients. Well, most of the time, anyway. There were always some patients who were guaranteed to irritate her and send her stress levels up, Mr Herring, a fussy and hypochondriacal frequent attender, being one of them, but in general she enjoyed seeing them all and even Mr Herring had been almost bearable after his vitamin overdose.

As she finished putting some routine blood results on the system, Callie turned to the next piece of paper on her to-do pile. It was Monica's blood test results and, as expected, they showed non-specific inflammation but nothing that gave Callie any idea as to what might be causing it.

Callie brought up the notes and checked them again. There was a copy of the letter that she had sent to the consultant, but no mention of any response, as yet. Callie knew that it would be several weeks before her patient was actually seen, but she sent off another letter to him, with the new blood test results, asking if he had any suggestion of what could be done to help Monica in the meantime. He might suggest some more specific tests that could be organised in the community. If so, Callie could save some time and get them done before he saw Monica, provided they weren't too expensive – she didn't want to incur the wrath of the senior partner.

Satisfied that she had done all she could, Callie continued her paperwork and even found time to complete some of her online training requirements. It might have been a boring morning, but it was one well spent. Glowing with self-righteousness, Callie decided to treat herself to a crab sandwich and a walk along the seafront as a reward before setting off on her afternoon visits.

* * *

There was a stiff breeze as Callie walked along the promenade and picked out a nice spot near the pier to stop and eat her sandwich. She loved to see the waves crashing against the pier supports and watch the antics of the seagulls as they rode the air currents. As long as they didn't get too close and try and steal her lunch. Everyone she knew had stories to tell of seagulls snatching food from their hands, or getting spattered with bird droppings. Seagulls were one of the hazards of living by the sea, but Callie wouldn't change it for the world.

Her mobile phone rang before she had a chance to even start eating and Callie answered it happily. Mike Parton had been on her list of people to call for an update so it was good that he was actually ringing her first; it saved her from feeling like she was nagging him.

"Hi, Mike, how can I help?" she asked brightly, but felt an immediate lurch in the pit of her stomach as he hesitated before answering. She knew that hesitation always meant bad news.

"Erm, the, um, Home Office pathologist has got back to us and said that he doesn't think the levels of potassium and chloride are high enough to suggest any foul play," Parton finally told her.

"What!" Callie shouted loud enough to startle the seagulls, and a few people walking along the seafront. "How can he have done the PM already?"

"He hasn't," Parton explained, "he has simply reviewed all the results provided by Dr Iqbal and given his opinion that there is nothing to suggest anything other than natural causes."

"Really?" Callie's voice had risen several octaves and she was gripping her mobile so tightly her knuckles were white and there was a risk of her breaking it. "I mean, really?" she repeated.

Parton didn't respond, probably because he didn't really know what to say to that. Callie took a deep breath; she wasn't helping anyone by getting hysterical.

"Okay." She could feel Parton's relief that she was getting herself under control. "You know Dr Iqbal and I disagree with him. So, what happens next?" she asked. "Or is that it?"

"Well, I have spoken to the coroner, and he will of course open an inquest as the death was unexpected."

Callie could hear the sub-context in his voice. The coroner would open an inquest, adjourn it until all the final reports were completed in a few months, and then almost certainly rule the cause of death as natural and close the inquest. End of story.

"You can't ask for a second opinion?"

"That was the second opinion."

"Third then, seeing as the two pathologists disagree?"

Parton hesitated again.

"Professor Wadsworth," he started, and Callie audibly groaned. "Wally" Wadsworth, as her godfather, one of Billy's predecessors, used to call the much-lauded Home Office pathologist when they disagreed over a cause of death.

"Professor Wadsworth," Parton repeated, well aware of what Callie thought of the man, "has said there is no need for further action, and I'm afraid that means no further action will be taken."

"The police?" she asked more in hope than expectation.

"Are not investigating, as no crime would seem to have been committed."

In truth, Callie knew they couldn't if no one thought anything illegal had happened. She closed her eyes in frustration.

"Have you contacted Billy?"

"No, but he was copied into the email I received."

"Thanks for letting me know, Mike." Callie quickly ended the call and hurried along the promenade. She had to get back home and pick up her car. She needed to see Billy. If she was upset by this, he would be devastated.

As she hurried up the steep steps to the top of the East Hill she thought about the night before and what she had said. Had she encouraged Billy in his belief that Mrs Mount had been killed? Would he have called it suspicious if she hadn't spoken to him about the strangeness of the scene where the old lady had been found, or the coincidence of Mr Darling being found in similar circumstances?

Callie was breathless when she reached the top and hurried across the clifftop towards her home and her car. She knew that she had influenced Billy, but equally, she knew that he would never have decided that there was anything wrong if he hadn't believed she was right. Billy was a grown man and a consummate professional. He knew his own mind, and while he respected her, he would not have been persuaded to report his concerns if he was not sure of them himself. He would not have jeopardised his future career in that way.

Blaming herself was simply not an option. Easy to say, harder for her to believe.

\* \* \*

When she had arrived at the hospital, where the mortuary was situated just out of sight of the main buildings, she had sat in the car for a few moments, trying to marshal her thoughts, thinking about how she should approach Billy, what he must be feeling, what she should say, could say, that might help. But in the end there was nothing for it; she just had to play it by ear, see him, speak to him and hope that she managed to find the right words. There was no point in putting it off any longer, so she had ventured into the underground world of the mortuary. As a frequent visitor, she had a pass that opened the main door; security everywhere in the hospital had got much tighter in recent years.

When Callie came out of the lift and entered the mortuary, it seemed quiet, but then it almost always was quiet. She felt that it was somehow more oppressive than usual, but knew that it was probably her feelings and imagination making it seem that way. She had a real dread that Billy was taking the news that he had been publicly contradicted badly. That even if she believed he had made his own decision, he would blame her.

As she walked along the brightly lit corridor, she jumped as a storeroom door opened and Jim, the heavily tattooed mortuary technician, came out.

"Dr Hughes," he said, unsmiling. That was a bad sign.

"Hello, Jim, is Dr Iqbal—" she nodded towards Billy's office.

"Yup," was Jim's tight reply before he turned and went back into the storeroom. Definitely not his normal cheerful chatty self.

44

Callie walked on and looked through the office door. She saw Billy at his desk, head in hands, staring into space.

"Hi there," she said gently as she went in.

He looked up.

"You heard then?"

She nodded and slid into the visitor's chair, reached out and put her hand over his.

"The good news is it looks like I won't be leaving the town just yet," he said.

"They've cancelled your appointment already?"

She knew that as contracts hadn't been signed yet, they would be able to do just that.

"No, they won't have got the news yet, but they will."

"Surely they won't decide against taking you on, just because you disagree with Wally Wadsworth."

Billy shrugged.

"If it was just a case of disagreeing, probably not, but he was being so patronising. I just saw red and may just possibly have told him exactly why he was wrong, and been, perhaps, a bit too insistent. Forthright even. He wasn't happy."

"He spoke to you." Callie was angry. No, she was livid.

Billy nodded.

"You've got to give him credit for that. He rang before sending the email. Professional courtesy, he said. Letting me know he was going to kneecap me before I got the official news." Billy sighed and rubbed his forehead. "And I lost it, pretty much called him dense for not seeing it my way. Maybe he's right, maybe I'm not cut out for this. Too inexperienced."

"Listen to me, Billy Iqbal, that pompous old windbag is well past his best. You are talented, hard-working and experienced, and he's just undermining you to make himself feel better."

There was the sound of clapping from the corridor. Jim was obviously listening in.

"I appreciate the vote of confidence, but you are both a bit biased." At least he was smiling now. It was a bit of a wobbly smile, but it was there.

"Only because we know you and how good you are, unlike the esteemed professor. He's got it wrong before, you know."

"You wouldn't think he'd ever made a bad call in his life if you'd heard him this morning."

Callie rubbed Billy's hand.

"It will be okay, and much as Jim and I don't want you to go, I'm sure your move will still be on if you want it to be."

He didn't seem convinced, and what did she know? He was probably right.

# Chapter 8

Callie had a headache the next morning, and as she walked across the clifftop to the steps that led down to Rock-a-Nore and the surgery, she reflected that it was entirely her own fault. Well, not entirely. She fully understood why Billy had wanted to go for a drink after work the evening before. He'd spent a large chunk of the afternoon on the phone to his prospective employers, who were going to have a meeting to discuss his appointment. It wasn't over, but it could be.

Billy didn't want to talk about it. He just wanted to drink enough to forget his ambitions or that he had ever wanted to be a Home Office pathologist like Professor Wadsworth – or better than him, as Callie had insisted he would be. The trouble was, the more he drank, the more he tortured himself over what had happened and what might have been. He was sure his career was over and no amount of reassurance from Callie would change his mind. Callie had to admit that he was probably right. Wadsworth would put the boot in; he was just that sort of person. So Callie had ended up drinking with Billy, keeping him company in his maudlin and depressed state and supporting him as best she could until closing time.

And that was why her head hurt and she felt faintly nauseous as she walked to work. It was a bright, sunshiny day and that should have lifted her spirits but instead it just made her eyes hurt.

Billy, irritatingly, had seemed fine when they woke up. No hangover – in fact he felt brighter having made the decision that "what will be, will be". If it was agreed that he could still take up his post in Northern Ireland, he would show them that they had made the right decision. If, however, they cancelled his appointment, more fool them. He would then have a choice: move abroad or carry on as a local pathologist in Hastings. He could maybe reapply to be a Home Office pathologist later, perhaps even get a post somewhere closer to Hastings once the professor had retired. After all, he couldn't go on forever, could he?

Callie had no idea how old the professor was, but he seemed to have been around for decades, sparring with Billy's predecessors, so yes, she thought he must be nearing retirement age.

"Are you sure I can't make you a bacon butty?" Billy had asked her as she sipped a mug of weak tea. Then, opening the fridge and seeing none in there, "Or I could buy you one on the way to work," he amended.

"No, no, I'm all right," she had insisted as she pulled on her coat. "I just need a brisk walk in the fresh air."

And it had been right, up to a point. It had given her time to go over the brighter front Billy had shown that morning. She wasn't fooled by it for a moment. He was still hurting inside, angry at himself as much as Wadsworth, but he had decided that there was nothing he could do to change what was going to happen. He had made his case to the representative of the Northern Ireland State Pathologist's unit and now he had to leave the decision to them. She wished she could be so calm and fatalistic. She was still seething that someone like Wally Wadsworth could destroy a good man so completely, and do it just because the person didn't afford him the respect he thought he was due.

All too soon, Callie was at the bottom of the cliff steps. It was only a short walk from there to her workplace, but she wasn't ready to face the world just yet; at least not the worlds inhabited by her patients. She wanted to think some more about Billy and his situation, if she could only get her head to clear a little.

Checking her watch, she decided she had time to walk through to the pebble beach for a blast of sea air. She would watch the waves until her head felt a little clearer, the cobwebs were blown away and her stomach had settled enough for her to contemplate a biscuit before facing her patients.

As she stood and looked out to sea, she knew that the Northern Ireland consortium would have little choice but to take back the job offer. Professor Wadsworth was a big cheese in the pathology world, and he would make sure they knew his opinion: Billy had made a mistake and had then compounded it by suggesting that he was right and that the great professor was wrong.

Callie should have felt pleased that at least he would stay, but she didn't want him to stay simply because his option to leave had gone. She wanted him to choose to stay, or at least ask her to go with him, even if she turned him down.

\* \* \*

Her morning surgery was long and she needed large amounts of coffee to get her through it. When lunchtime finally arrived, her hangover was mostly gone and had left her feeling ravenous. She craved carbs and grease and salt and set off for her favourite café on the High Street, mouth already watering at the thought of crispy bacon. Her mobile rang when she was halfway there and she was surprised to see that the call was from Miller.

"Hiya," she answered warily, "I'm just about to go into the Land of Green Ginger." She had used the café as a meeting place on several occasions with Miller in the past, so she knew he would know where she was. The cosy and almost homely atmosphere in the café, along with the wonderful food served there, made it a regular haunt.

He asked her to order him the Full English with a double portion of bubble and squeak and said he would be there in fifteen minutes. She smiled. Although she knew very well that he was going to tell her that he was dropping any sort of enquiry into Mrs Mount and Mr Darling, she also knew that he had no choice but to do so, and at least he was planning on telling her in person.

The Land of Green Ginger was fortunately not full and Callie was able to get a table by the window so that she could watch for Miller. It wasn't long before she saw him striding along the High Street. He gave a little wave as he saw her and quickly came in.

"I love this place," he said a little later as he scraped the last of the juices up with a piece of toast.

"Me too," Callie agreed, looking at her own plate. It wasn't quite as clean as Miller's but she'd eaten far more than she usually did at lunchtime. She had a faint twinge of guilt as she thought of all the calories, not to mention all the fat and salt and other bad things she had just eaten, but it didn't last long. It wasn't like she made a habit of eating unhealthily; far from it. In fact, the waitress had looked surprised at the change to her usual order of smoked salmon with either scrambled eggs or avocado, but had not commented other than a slightly raised eyebrow. She understood. Everyone knew that a fried breakfast was the only thing you should eat after a heavy night drinking.

There had been no further discussion of the two deaths once he had told her firmly that he was closing the case, and they had concentrated on their food. Callie had also given Miller a few surreptitious looks. He seemed well; no signs of stress or tiredness. He looked as if he had put on a bit of weight too; not a lot, but his face had filled out slightly. Perhaps his wife was back, although she had always tended to cause him as much if not more stress than his job, Callie thought. So maybe her leaving him had turned out to be a good thing.

"What are you going to do?" he asked once they had both sat back, replete.

"This afternoon? I have a couple of visits and then evening surgery followed by a riveting evening meeting of the LMC."

Miller would have no idea that LMC stood for Local Medical Committee, a group representing local GPs. Their meetings certainly tended not to be riveting, or even particularly interesting, Callie thought, but she went along for the chance to meet with other GPs in the town and catch up on all the gossip.

"I mean about the two deaths."

She had known that, of course.

"I mean, you still think there's something suspicious about them, don't you?" he asked.

"Yes, don't you?"

"I have to admit they do seem a bit weird, and it would be good to know why there was that bruising to Mrs Mount's arm but it doesn't mean there's anything criminal going on."

"It's still criminal if someone did something wrong and is now trying to cover their tracks."

"You think the nurse might have given her an injection and then denied it when she died?"

Callie gave it some thought, then shook her head.

"I don't know. It's not usual for a nurse to be giving IV drugs to patients like that. To be frank, we don't do much of it in the community at all, unless we are talking long-term or terminal care, where a lot of drugs will need to be given that way. In those cases, we, or the hospital, put in special ports or lines for the drugs to be given. I just can't see why the nurse, or anyone for that matter, would be giving an IV injection directly into a vein like that, it's too risky. If the needle slips, or the patient moves, you would end up injecting into the surrounding tissue. Of course, she might well take blood from there, but not give anything."

"So, the bruise might just be from taking blood?"

"Yes." Callie knew where he was headed.

"Is it possible that the nurse took the blood, maybe was a bit rough, and the patient died, not because of the nurse being rough, but just did, and the nurse then tried to cover it up? In case she caused the woman to die?"

"Well, I don't see that taking blood could cause so much stress that she died, but theoretically, yes, she could have just upped and died while the nurse was taking blood. And yes, I can see that the nurse might be anxious about being blamed so then denied doing it."

Miller held his hands out, palm up in a "there you go" gesture.

"But, no one had asked her to take blood," Callie persisted. "So why would she?"

"People make mistakes and then they panic afterwards."

"Yes, but…" She couldn't really think of anything to refute this. He was right. Generally, she did believe more in cock-ups than conspiracies, but was that what this was? She wasn't convinced.

"So, I return to my previous question, what are you going to do?"

"Doesn't seem to be much I can do."

"Good." He stood up. "Not that that's ever stopped you in the past."

And she knew he was right. And it wasn't going to stop her now. She just wasn't exactly sure what she was going to do. Yet.

# Chapter 9

As expected, the LMC meeting that evening looked like it was going to be less than riveting. It was being held in a utilitarian room in a local community hall because they didn't charge, Callie presumed, as she couldn't think of any other reason why they would use a room that was always guaranteed to be too hot in summer and freezing in winter.

A speaker had been arranged to talk about annual targets that evening, again, so Callie ensured that she arrived too late for most of his mind-numbingly boring talk. She wasn't the only one; there were even a few of her colleagues who had successfully timed their arrival to make sure that they missed it altogether.

The second part of the meeting was the social section and a good opportunity for Callie to mix with her fellow GPs from the town and surrounding area over a glass of warm apple juice. Some of her colleagues were braving the cheap plonk, but Callie was strict about not drinking and driving. Her work with the police meant that she saw the consequences all too often. She was called in to take blood far less often these days, not because fewer people were being caught, but because they rarely insisted on a blood test anymore and there was no need for a doctor to be present when they used the breathalyser. It was yet another way that the need for a police doctor was slowly but surely being eroded. If it carried on, she might find herself with only her GP role left, whether that was what she wanted or not.

She looked around to see who she knew. Angus was there, being charmingly vague as usual, and so was his wife, Caroline, who was never vague and rarely charming but a very good doctor nonetheless.

"Hi, Caroline," Callie said as she approached her just as she was pouring herself some orange juice. "How's things?"

"Fine, fine. Listen." Caroline picked up her drink and grabbed Callie by the elbow, pulling her away from the crowd at the drinks table. "Dr Iqbal contacted me to discuss that patient of mine who was found in similar circumstances to Angus's."

"I know. I hope that was okay with you?"

"Of course. Did anything come of it? I'm kicking myself for not having called you in at the time."

"Enquiries are ongoing," Callie replied, not entirely truthfully, but not entirely untruthfully, either. She was still making enquiries, after all, even if no one else was. "And you had no real reason to be suspicious, it's just the second one that makes me think something might be wrong. In fact, I thought I'd discreetly ask around and see if anyone else had had any similar cases."

"Bugger discreet, why don't you—" Caroline turned round and, direct as ever, grabbed a man standing behind them by the wrist. "Donald, Dr Hughes here needs to ask everyone about an unusual case, see if there have been others, can she address the room?"

And so, Callie found herself standing at the front and telling all her fellow GPs about the two cases, and how these elderly people were found dead in their chairs, all dressed up with nowhere to go. She was honest in that she admitted that they had no way of knowing if the deaths were connected or if they were even suspicious, but that, at least in the second case, there were some unanswered questions. Then she asked them to speak to her if they had seen anything similar, and there was an embarrassing silence in response.

A woman who Callie thought was in her late twenties or possibly early thirties, was standing at the back, right in the corner of the room, trying not to look at her whilst simultaneously glancing over at an older man, who Callie recognised from previous meetings as a local doctor, but whom she didn't actually know. The older doctor looked as if he might say something but then changed his mind.

Callie quickly realised that no one was going to speak up while the meeting was in progress. They would not want to admit to having missed a suspicious death, and they certainly wouldn't want to do so in front of their colleagues.

"You don't have to say anything here and now, of course," she amended, with an encouraging smile. "Perhaps, if you know of anything you think might fit with these, you could contact me? Or if you know of any other odd events that you think might be connected? You can talk to me later tonight or send me an email, leave a message at the surgery, whatever suits you best."

Callie looked round for the man she had seen, because she was pretty sure he knew something, but disappointingly, she couldn't see him anywhere. She went over to the drinks table but no one rushed up to speak to her after that; in fact, they all seemed to be avoiding her in case anyone thought they knew anything about the deaths, so, having spoken to a few other people she knew, Callie headed for the door.

As she walked across the car park, there was a movement to her left and she turned to see the woman who had been at the back of the room. She was wearing her coat and had clearly been waiting for Callie to come out.

"Dr Hughes?" The woman was looking nervously at the main door, checking to see if anyone else was coming out.

"Yes," Callie answered her and allowed herself to be led further into the car park, where they couldn't be seen by the people still inside. "How can I help?"

"My training supervisor told me not to speak to you, but" – she looked round, as if seeking inspiration – "I don't know what to do."

"I appreciate it's hard but if you have any information that might be pertinent, speaking to me is the right thing to do," Callie encouraged her.

She had already decided the woman must be a trainee as she didn't recognise her. She remembered that the man she had been looking at was a training GP, so it made sense.

"I don't want it to get back to him."

"I'm not sure I can promise that it won't." Callie felt she had to be honest. "I mean, if there's any kind of investigation, he's going to realise that someone spoke to us."

The woman chewed her lip, she was clearly torn.

"Look, if he's trying to stop you talking to me, he's the one in the wrong here," Callie told her. "It really shouldn't impact on you and your training position."

The woman snorted.

"He's already made it clear he doesn't think I'm good enough. This will just finish things off."

"It's only a few months until you rotate to another position."

"I know, but I don't think I can take it, even for just a short time."

"If it helps, I'll speak to the person who organised the training, see if we can get you transferred to another practice."

"I tried and they told me that it's really hard to change and to stick it out."

Callie suspected that it had more to do with them not wanting to be bothered.

"I know it's always difficult to get a new training place if one doesn't work out," she said firmly. "But it's not impossible. You have to tell them you can't stay."

The woman took a deep breath.

"What if he's right and I'm useless? Maybe, I should just give up." There was a break in her voice and a tear tracked down her cheek, but she seemed oblivious to it.

"Don't do that, please." Callie was angry now. How dare one of her colleagues bully this woman to the point where she was thinking of giving up? "We need all the doctors we can get."

Callie fished a packet of tissues out of her bag and offered the woman one, and then waited patiently while she blew her nose and got her feelings under control.

"What's your name?"

"Eleanor. Eleanor Sweeting."

"And who is your training supervisor?"

The woman hesitated before answering.

"Dr Richardson," she finally told Callie. "Do you know him?"

"I can't say that I do, really," Callie replied.

She remembered speaking to him at some function or other and he had come across as generally quite nice and funny, but when she thought more, she realised that some of his remarks were quite cutting, unkind even, in the way he talked about people, patients, colleagues, whoever, even if what he said was true. He'd certainly come across as someone who didn't suffer fools gladly.

"He's always putting me down. Tells me I'm not cut out to be a GP, but it's what I've always wanted to do, to be." Eleanor sniffed again and Callie touched her on her shoulder.

"Perhaps a female GP would be a better trainer for you."

"Do you—?"

"Not qualified to do it, sorry," Callie said quickly. She had far too many other things going on with her police work to supervise a trainee, let alone do all the paperwork that it entailed, so she had never taken the necessary qualifications to enable her to be a training supervisor.

"Oh well." Eleanor blew her nose again.

"But we do take on trainees in our practice."

Callie knew that Hugh Grantham, the senior partner and only qualified trainer at the practice wouldn't be happy with her suggesting this young woman could move to him, even if he didn't have a student at the moment. He had declined to have one because he was trying to cut down on the amount of work he did in preparation for retirement in a few years' time. No one else had volunteered to take his place. Oh, well, needs must, Callie told herself, and was pleased to see the woman visibly brighten at the thought that she might be able to move elsewhere. Callie crossed her fingers and hoped she wouldn't have to let Eleanor down if Hugh Grantham refused to take her on.

"So, about this patient he didn't want you to tell me about?" she prompted.

"Oh, yes, of course. It was a woman I went to visit about a month ago. Just a routine visit. She had diabetes and other problems, dementia, poor mobility and so on. Lived in the mobile home park, you know the one?"

Callie nodded.

"When I got there, there was no answer, so I looked through the window and could see her, sitting in the chair. I knocked again and when she didn't move, I tried the door and it was unlocked so I went in. It was just so weird."

"In what way?"

"Well, like you said, there was a suitcase by the door. One of those little wheelie ones you can take on the plane as hand luggage. Her handbag was on top of it, with her coat neatly hung over the handle. All ready to go. And she was sitting there, in a chair facing the door, dead."

"Was her death expected?"

"Well, it wasn't unexpected, if you know what I mean. Dr Richardson was happy to sign the death certificate. I mean, there was nothing suspicious. It was just odd."

"Why didn't he want you to speak to me?"

"I suppose he doesn't want you questioning his opinion that it was a natural death, as he was the one who signed the certificate," she answered. "In case the relatives make a fuss, or something, I suppose."

"She had children?"

"No. But I think there was a niece. I assumed June, the dead woman, had been packed ready to go and stay with her. I really didn't think any more about it, until just now, when you told us about the others."

Eleanor looked up anxiously as a few people came out of the meeting, calling goodbye to each other, and started heading for their cars.

"She probably was going to her niece's and there isn't any connection, but it wouldn't hurt to check." Callie tried to reassure Eleanor.

Callie quickly noted down both Eleanor's and the patient's details, and promised she would look into the possibility of her moving to Callie's surgery to complete this section of her training.

There was nothing for it, Callie told herself as she finally got into her car to leave; she would have to make an impassioned plea to Dr Grantham in the morning, and then he would have to go to the training organisers and persuade them, too. It wouldn't reflect well on Dr Richardson, but then, that was his own fault. Callie just hoped that Dr Richardson was wrong about Eleanor being useless and that she turned out to be a good doctor. If she wasn't, Dr Grantham would never let Callie forget it.

As she drove out of the community centre car park, Callie saw Dr Richardson come out of the front door and look around as if searching for someone. She hoped the trainee had already left – she was in no state to handle any further criticism. The thought of Dr Richardson upsetting the poor woman hardened Callie's resolve. She would talk to Dr Grantham in the morning.

# Chapter 10

Callie stood outside Hugh Grantham's consulting room with a cup of his favourite coffee in one hand and a plate of plain chocolate digestives in the other.

"Bribery, is it?" Marie, one of the practice nurses, asked as she passed, nicking a biscuit off the plate before knocking on the door and opening it for Callie, all in one smooth movement. She was gone before Callie could respond, with either a complaint or a thank you.

"Do you have a minute, Hugh?" Callie entered the consulting room, placing the cup and the plate on his desk before closing the door.

He eyed her suspiciously.

"Do I have a choice?"

"I could take these away and have them myself," she said with a smile.

"Sit, sit. Something tells me I will regret it, but–" A twinkle in his eye belied his words.

"I wanted to talk about a trainee," she said as she sat and placed her offerings in front of him.

"I don't have one at the moment."

"I know, but–"

"Because I really don't have the time."

"I know, but—"

"It wouldn't be fair on the trainee."

"I know, but—"

"And I don't want one."

"Dr Richardson is bullying his trainee."

"Bullying is a strong word."

"There's no other word for it. And he's doing it to the extent that she is considering giving up, Hugh. And that's just plain wrong."

Dr Grantham stopped to take a sip of his coffee and collect his thoughts.

"I concede that Dr Richardson can be a little, um, abrasive."

"You should have seen her at the LMC meeting, Hugh, she was in tears."

Hugh Grantham sighed in resignation.

"Give me her details. I'll speak to her and if she really wants to do this, I'll speak to the area organiser, but that doesn't mean it's a done deal."

Callie beamed. She had won and it had been easier than she expected. Perhaps Dr Grantham had had a run in with Dr Richardson before.

\* \* \*

Buoyed by her easy victory with Dr Grantham, Callie called Mike Parton to check that he was in his office. On finding he was, she told him to stay put as she was coming straight round to see him. She knew he wouldn't really want to speak to her, because he would know exactly what she wanted to speak to him about, but she also knew that he was a decent man and would wait. He would never try and avoid her, even if he knew he was going to disappoint her.

Callie did think about taking a bribe with her in the form of some kind of delicacy from the bakery, but decided he really wasn't the sort of man who would be open to bribery of any kind. His formal, almost funereal manner made many describe him as a cold fish, but Callie knew better. He was a good man who dealt with death on a daily basis, and handled it, and those affected by it, with dignity, kindness and understanding.

Parton smiled as she came into his office and offered her a chair.

Knowing that he was likely to be busy, Callie didn't waste time before getting down to business.

"I know you can't do anything about getting the police to investigate the two deaths we talked about, not now Dr Wadsworth has given his opinion, but I wondered, if I spoke to the coroner, do you think he might ask for further investigation through the medical examiner?"

The medical examiner post was a relatively new one, part of a national programme to look into deaths and death certification after Dr Harold Shipman had managed to get away with killing his patients for so long. The medical examiner was based at the regional hospital and his remit was fairly wide-ranging, looking at death certification and hopefully alerting the authorities to any anomalies such as a cluster of unexplained deaths, or rising drug mortality. Even though she didn't personally know the examiner who covered Hastings, as he was based in Brighton, Callie was sure that if he heard there were concerns from two different sources, he would be persuaded that this situation was worth a second look.

Parton gave her request the thought it deserved.

"I don't think so, but I will make the suggestion. Um," he hesitated, "I understand Dr Iqbal may have spoken to the medical examiner already, and been told that he didn't think there was enough evidence to warrant an investigation."

That was news to Callie; she hadn't realised that Billy was on the same track.

"You could also tell him that I may have found a third case, if you think that might sway him."

"A third?"

"I don't have the full particulars yet, but the case was brought up at the LMC meeting last night."

Callie didn't want to name the patient, or the doctor involved at this stage, because of the delicate situation with the trainee, but she was hopeful that mention of a third case might get the coroner's attention and make him think he ought to be looking at the cases proactively rather than waiting for more deaths to occur.

"I think he might be inclined to speak to the medical examiner if there is a third." It seemed Parton was convinced anyway. "If you can get the patient details to me as soon as possible?"

Callie knew that as soon as he had a name, Parton would be able to check whether or not there had been a post-mortem and what had been the method of disposal. If exhumation was difficult, that was nothing compared to getting any further information after a body had been cremated. She also knew that he would check with the patient's own doctor, to see if he was concerned about the death. Unfortunately, Callie didn't think Dr Richardson would say he was.

"Of course, as soon as I have all the details, I'll get them to you. He can tell the examiner I'm happy to be contacted directly as well." Callie just wanted the coroner to get things under way.

Parton cleared his throat and Callie knew that he was about to say something unpalatable.

"Of course, it would be easier to persuade him if the details came from someone other than yourself."

"Why?" Callie looked at Parton in surprise.

"Because the coroner is not unaware of the situation between yourself and Dr Iqbal and also how Dr Wadsworth's opinion has affected him."

Callie was about to protest that Billy had absolutely nothing to do with how or why she was pushing for further investigation, but she knew, as did both Parton and the coroner, that it was not true. Without Billy's involvement, she would still have hoped for further investigation, but she wouldn't have pushed so hard for it, or been so sure that he was right. She desperately wanted to save Billy's career, and that inevitably was colouring her view of the matter. So she kept quiet.

"Can you get the patient's own doctor to bring the case to the coroner's attention?"

"Of course," Callie said, knowing full well that that would not be possible. Not unless she could persuade Eleanor to bring the case forward and even that wouldn't work if Dr Richardson denied the situation, or said his trainee was misremembering the event. Perhaps Caroline or Angus should raise their concerns? She'd speak to them.

"I'll get them to contact you as soon as possible."

She smiled and wondered how long she could reasonably hold Parton and the coroner off, and if they would start to move things forward while they waited. She certainly hoped so, because she wasn't sure she would ever get the information they needed.

Not unless someone else died, that was.

# Chapter 11

"You spoke to the medical examiner?" Callie was more stating a fact than asking Billy, as she already knew from Parton that he had.

"Yes," he said and looked dubiously at the saucepan she was stirring in a desultory way. He was right to look concerned; she had sort of followed the recipe, substituting items when she realised that she didn't have them, hopefully with something similar. The result did not look entirely appetising, she had to admit. And it didn't smell too good either.

"And?"

"He wasn't keen to get involved at this stage."

Billy grabbed a beer from the fridge and went over to the large window. He was pretending to be looking at the amazing view of the old town as the sun went down, but Callie wasn't fooled for a minute.

"Had Wadsworth been onto him, then?"

"Almost certainly." Billy sighed, concern etched in his face.

"It will be okay," she said and went over to him, put her arms round him and rested her head on his shoulder. Recent rain meant that the houses below them seemed to twinkle as lights were switched on. It was a sight that never failed to enchant Callie, but she didn't think that Billy was seeing it at all. He was too busy fretting about his future. And who could blame him?

As she watched more and more lights appear in the evening gloom, she stroked Billy's arm and was rewarded by feeling him slowly relax. He kissed the top of her head and took a swig of his beer.

"Maybe it's for the best," he said, although he didn't sound convinced.

Callie tilted her chin up and they kissed, a long slow kiss. Until Billy suddenly pulled away.

"Is something wrong?" she asked and then she smelled it too: dinner burning.

Callie hurried into the open-plan kitchen area and grabbed the saucepan. Billy came up behind her and looked over her shoulder. There was a mix of crispy, burnt lumps of chicken in a sludgy, lumpy blackened sauce, all stuck to the bottom of the pan.

"Would you be very upset if I said I didn't really want to eat that?"

"No, because that would make two of us," Callie answered as she chucked it all, including the saucepan, in the bin and closed the lid with a clang.

"Takeaway? Or would you rather go out, my dearest domestic goddess?" Billy asked her, unable to hide a smile.

Callie sighed. She somehow doubted she was ever going to be a good cook, or even a passable one, so why did she keep pretending?

"Oh, go on then, let's have a takeaway," she answered. At least her culinary disaster had cheered him up.

Later, once they had finished eating their pizza and Billy had drunk a couple more beers, they talked again of the future and what, if anything, they could do to take back control of it. As she snuggled up against him on the sofa, Callie told him about the possible third case, and how she didn't think it was enough to persuade the coroner.

"Not without support from the GP anyway, and that's not likely," she explained.

Even if she managed to get Eleanor moved across to her own practice, Dr Richardson would have to add his support to her contention that his patient was another victim, and if he hadn't wanted to tell her about the patient in the first place, he was unlikely to do so once he had lost his trainee. He would have to admit that he had made a wrong call on a patient's death, which could happen to anyone, after all. However, if it got out that he'd been bullying his trainee, he could be taken off the approved trainer list. She couldn't see him being happy about that.

"Sadly," Billy said, "our best hope is for there to be another victim." Callie loved him for the fact that he couldn't bring himself to sound enthusiastic about the prospect. Another death would be another life cut short, or at least a little shorter, even if it saved his career.

"What do we think is actually going on?" Callie asked him, and herself, as she made herself a cup of coffee and fetched a beer for Billy. "I mean, are we really thinking that someone is going round killing off old people?"

"One person dead from an injection of potassium chloride could be an accident, or negligence, but−"

"We don't know if either of the others died that way, though." Callie was waving her glass around to emphasise her point and was in danger of splashing wine everywhere. "All we do know is that they died in their chairs, with a packed suitcase at their sides."

"True," Billy agreed. Callie hadn't kept count of how many beers he had had, but she was sure it was quite a few. "But there's nothing illegal about organising holidays."

"So why would this person do it?"

"Perhaps they aren't."

"What do you mean?"

"Well, they don't have to be real holidays, as the victims are never going to go on them."

"That's very true. So, the holiday story is just to cheer them up, do you think? Give them a happy death?"

"It could be, couldn't it, if it's some kind of mercy killing?"

She gave that some thought.

"But these weren't people who were suffering too badly with their health, as far as I can tell. They were elderly, of course and had their fair share of illnesses, but not terminal ones, or particularly painful ones, as far as I know."

"Maybe you could get as many details about them as possible, see if there are any links or similarities? You never know, a reason why they were killed may come up."

Callie agreed, but that was easier said than done. Eleanor would have to be her source of information on June, the third victim. That was assuming Eleanor could be persuaded to say anything, as she could be laying herself open to accusations of breaking patient confidentiality rules, even if the patient was dead. Callie was acutely aware that she should take care, as she didn't want to end the poor woman's career before it had really started.

On the others, she was sure Caroline and Angus would co-operate; after all, they had alerted her to the problem in the first place.

"I'll see what I can do," she told him as she took his beer bottle and put it on the table, "but meanwhile, the bedroom beckons."

He smiled.

* * *

Next morning, nursing a renewed sense of purpose, Callie set about her task of finding out more about the three deaths. She left messages with Angus, Caroline and Eleanor, asking them all to let her have anything they felt able to in view of the confidentiality issues. Ideally, she would have liked access to their full patient notes, so that she could trawl through them for anything of relevance, but she knew that was unlikely, particularly in Eleanor's case. She added that she expected them all to consult their legal representatives to ensure what they were doing was right, but she also pointed out that if the case was taken up by the medical examiner, as she had requested, they would have to do it anyway.

She had debated giving them this piece of information, as it might make the lawyers advise them to wait until the examiner was on board, but she had decided to be as open as possible. As she had told Billy the night before, she still had to work with these people, so she needed to be fair to them from the start.

Callie also asked them to write down everything they remembered about finding the bodies: what the patients were wearing, the suitcases, anything unexpected. She felt that this type of information would not be subject to confidentiality rules to the same degree. For her own part, Callie did as she asked of them, and started to set out an account of everything she remembered from that first scene.

She described as much of the details as she could: the people there, including the surly nurse, the nosy neighbour and the taxi driver; although she couldn't remember the taxi company name, she wrote down everything she could think of, just in case.

Then she wrote down everything she had been told by Angus, Caroline and Eleanor so that she could compare it against whatever they sent back to her.

Callie then followed her account by writing down a series of questions.

Question one: were they all visited by a community nurse team? If so, who was on those teams?

It wasn't that Callie had taken an instant dislike to the nurse whom she had met at Mrs Mount's home, because she had come across her on several occasions, and the woman had always been abrupt to the point of rudeness and Callie had never seen her smile. Callie didn't seriously consider her to be a mass murderer; it was more that she might be the perpetrator of petty unkindness on her clientele. If the ruse of the holidays was to make the old people happy, Callie didn't think this particular nurse would bother. Several of Callie's patients had complained about minor events: being rough, rude or deliberately leaving items out of reach, but being uncaring, or even malicious didn't make you a murderer. Necessarily. Either way, Callie knew that she needed to talk to Judy or Jenny or whatever her name was, again, if only to find out more about the victim, and she wasn't exactly looking forward to it.

Question two: why did they all seem to think they were going away? And if they really were (unlikely in Callie's mind), who had organised it? Social services, a charity organisation, a church group?

Callie couldn't honestly believe that social services did organise events like that but at least she had a contact in the organisation who might be able to help with information. Callie wrote herself a note to call Helen Austen, the senior social worker she knew.

Question three: was it possible that they were all due to be picked up by the same taxi firm? The firm was unlikely to be involved because the car would inevitably turn up after the event, but they might have information about the person who had booked them. It was unfortunate that Callie couldn't actually remember the name of the firm who had sent a car to collect Mrs Mount. She would have to look through the local websites and adverts in the paper to see if she recognised the logo.

Question four, the biggest question of all: why?

For the life of her, Callie could not think of a reason why anyone would want to kill off a bunch of random old people. None of them seemed to have had much money, love seemed unlikely, and the murders, if that was what they were, seemed to have been planned rather than acts of rage. She just hoped some sort of motive became apparent as she answered some of the other questions and got to know more about the victims and any connections there might be. But motive wasn't really important in the greater scheme of things. What she needed to do was collect enough connections and evidence to convince the police that the victims had been unlawfully killed. Then she could leave it to the police to search out the motive and perpetrator. She just had to get them on board.

\* \* \*

The third patient on Callie's morning list was Monica Claydon. Whilst she was waiting for her to make her way to the consulting room, Callie checked her notes. There was nothing new from the consultant and Monica hadn't been asked to attend because of any abnormal tests, or for review.

"Hello," Callie said as Monica came into the room and sat down with a small sigh. She certainly looked no better than the last time she had been to see Callie. If anything, she looked worse. Callie thought about asking what she could do to help, or why Monica had come to the surgery, but decided to let her patient do the talking, so she just smiled and waited.

"I don't know what to do with myself, Dr Hughes, and that's the truth." There was no doubt that Monica looked and sounded exhausted. "Everywhere hurts; my joints, my back, my head. The pills worked for a while but now don't seem to do anything."

Callie checked what she had prescribed previously and knew there was little else she could try.

"Have you heard back from the hospital?" she asked.

Monica held out a sheet of paper.

"I got an appointment but it's not until the end of next month." She shook her head. "That is a long time to feel like this."

Callie knew she was right, but equally knew that it was actually about average for a first appointment with rheumatology. She also knew that it wouldn't help Monica to tell her that.

"I'll give them a call and see if we can't get you in earlier," Callie told her. She knew that the chances were slim, but felt that Monica needed to feel that people were at least trying to help her. With that little bit of reassurance, and hope, Monica left and Callie had to make a decision.

She could try ringing the clerks who worked in appointments, but they would be unlikely to be able to help, even if they wanted to, because of the strict rules in place to prevent them from prioritising one patient over another. The consultant's secretary could change her place on the list, but would only do that with the consultant's approval. So, in effect, the only person who could move Monica up the waiting list was the consultant himself and Callie had to balance irritating him by asking him to do that, against the prospect of letting Monica down when she had promised to help.

In reality, it was no contest. Callie always put her patients first, so she made the call, and was gratified when the consultant agreed to try and see Monica sooner and said he would ask his secretary to organise it. The chances were that he would forget, but just having that promise gave Callie the ammunition she needed to then ring the secretary herself and get her to remind him that he had agreed to it.

It all took time, and there was no guarantee that her hard work would make the slightest bit of difference, because for every patient that was moved up the list, someone had to be moved down and it wasn't fair on them. The consultant and secretary might review the list and decide that Monica wasn't any more urgent than those in front of her and that she would have to wait. In an overloaded system, someone always lost out, but she had done all she could to make sure it wasn't Monica.

* * *

It never ceased to amaze Callie that Helen Austen could work effectively in an office that was such a tip, but even by Helen's standards things seemed to be worse than usual. Great heaps of files threatened to spill onto the floor, and letters, both opened and unopened, covered the desk. The phone was on top of some half-filled forms and barely stopped ringing the entire time Callie was in the room. She had to restrain herself from answering it, because Helen seemed happy to just let it ring and talk over the noise. Callie hated to think of the poor people leaving messages, as she had done earlier to say she was coming to see the social worker. It seemed that Helen didn't even get around to listening to them as she had been surprised to see Callie when she turned up.

"It's absolute mayhem at the moment," Helen explained unnecessarily, as she searched through the new letters that had just been delivered to her desk before putting them all in her overflowing in-tray, where they would probably stay forever. Callie hoped she was dealing with the email copies faster, but knew it was unlikely.

"One of my team has been suspended because a client made a complaint and half the others have gone off sick because of the stress of having to cover her work," Helen continued. "And what with the vacancies as well, I'm currently covering five full-time posts." She sat back in her chair and sighed. "So, what can I do for you?"

"Gosh, Helen, I'm really sorry to bother you like this, I know you rarely have time for a break so—" Callie put down the takeaway cup of coffee she had brought for the social worker and fished out the almond croissant she had bought to go with it.

"You are my best friend and I love you." Helen almost groaned with pleasure as she took a bite of the pastry. "Thank you and if this" — she waved the croissant at the coffee — "is a bribe, that's fine. I am open to bribery."

"It's just a small offering in return for your expertise. I have a question."

"Ask away."

"I wanted to find out about holidays for elderly patients. Where would you go to arrange something like that?"

"Do you mean respite care? Join the queue."

"No, an actual holiday."

"No idea." Helen thought between bites of croissant and sips of coffee. "Saga? Charities? Church?"

"But you, by which I mean social care, don't organise them at all?"

"God, no," she laughed. "Believe me, I'd love to send some of these old dears away for a bit, but we don't do that. Can't. Budget just wouldn't allow for it, and can you imagine the paperwork? All it would take is for one of them to wander off and I'd be filling out forms for the rest of my life." She shook her head. "There's no way. I wouldn't even get beyond the risk assessment level."

"So, you don't know of anyone who is specifically offering holidays to elderly people round here?"

"No, but if there is someone, let me know and I'll happily recommend a few potential customers."

All in all, it wasn't a very satisfactory outcome, but it confirmed what Callie had thought, that whoever was promising to take these pensioners away, it wasn't anyone official. She'd have to spend some time ringing round churches and charities, pretending to arrange a holiday for her elderly mother and see if anyone said they provided that sort of service. But first, she'd have to make a list of who to call, and she had a feeling that would take almost as long as the calls themselves.

With a sigh, she headed back to the surgery.

# Chapter 12

"Honestly, I had no idea just how many church groups and charities there were in Hastings."

Callie and Kate were sitting at their usual table in The Stag, underneath the mummified cat display. Kate was drinking a pint of bitter and Callie was sipping a spritzer, much to Kate's disgust. She had called her friend a lightweight when Callie had said that she really didn't feel like drinking and asked for a sparkling water. In the end, after much teasing about how talking to all these church groups had ended with her signing the pledge and joining the Salvation Army, Callie had given way and ordered a white wine spritzer. She planned to keep topping it up with soda so that it got progressively weaker during the evening.

"So, what are you going to do now you have your list of churches and charities," Kate asked. "Ring them all and ask if they, or any of their helpers, are killing people off?"

"No," Callie replied patiently. "I'm going to ask them if they arrange holidays for pensioners because my elderly, mildly confused mother needs to go away for a break."

"Diana will love being referred to as elderly and mildly confused."

"Which is why she must never find out that I have taken her name in vain."

"Won't they just suggest you take her yourself?"

"I've thought of that. I'm going to say I have to go into hospital for a while and she won't like people coming into her home to help care for her, so I thought it would be a good time for her to go away."

"But what if they want to contact her?"

"I'll cross that bridge when I come to it." A bit of Callie thought that her mother might relish playing a role in one of her investigations, having always been a keen member of the local amateur dramatic society. It would give her something to talk about at her bridge sessions as well, but Callie knew that her father would never forgive her if she put her mother at risk, so she would have to take great care not to do that.

"I could play an old lady. I could pretend to be your mother." Kate had a twinkle in her eye.

"There is no way you could convince anyone you were old and decrepit." Callie told her with a laugh. Kate was always brimming with life and vitality.

"But I could be confused," she laughed, "in fact, I often am."

Kate jiggled her nearly empty pint glass at Callie's almost full tumbler.

"Is it my round?" Callie asked.

"No, mine. And I'm going to get a refill. Do you have room for another spritzer, or perhaps a glass of water? Perked up with a squirt of lime juice?"

\* \* \*

Callie had to admit that Kate had a point as she sat down with her list later that evening and prepared to start on the phone calls. Whilst she might find a few places that were willing to admit they might help her aged mother have a holiday, if she wanted to get further than that she would have to give them more details, which could be problematic. Another problem, as she quickly found out, was that most places were closed out of office hours, and even if her call was answered, it wasn't by anyone who could help her. She spoke to a lot of cleaners who didn't have the answers to her questions. This was definitely a job for the daytime, which was going to add to her difficulties.

Frustrated by her lack of progress, Callie turned her efforts to taxi firms in Hastings. A quick Google search got her a list of all the main firms and she then went to their websites. A few she could dismiss straight away because she would have recognised the colourful or distinctive logos on the cars. She was sure there was nothing like that on the taxi she had seen at Mrs Mount's. Her problem was that quite a few taxi firms just had their name and a telephone number on the side of their cars, as she remembered, and they were in no way distinctive. And that was before she got to all the smaller one-man-and-his-car firms that didn't even have websites. She was going to have to call round the twenty or so numbers of the companies she couldn't eliminate and see if she could get anyone to admit to having been booked to collect Mrs Mount and take her to the bus station.

Starting with number one on her list, Callie gave them a call.

"Good evening, Old Town Cars, how can I help you?"

The response time had been only a couple of rings so Callie made a mental note to use them if she needed a taxi in future; not that she would, because pretty much everywhere that she went in Hastings, apart from work, was within walking distance.

"Hello, my name is Dr Hughes and I work with the police," she told them. "I'm ringing to find out if you had a pick-up for a Mrs Mount from St Peter's Road near the park on—"

"I'm sorry," the call-handler cut in, "we are not allowed to give out any personal information about our clients."

"I'm with the police and I just want you to confirm or deny whether or not you were booked for this journey from St Peter's Road to the bus station on the first."

"I'm sorry, but you will need to go through official channels to get that information. I am not allowed to say anything unless authorised. Good evening."

There was a click as the handler hung up. Callie sighed in frustration and moved on to the next number on her list, to be met with a very similar attitude.

The calls to all the larger firms got a fairly predictable response in that they refused to give her any information unless she had a warrant, which wasn't going to happen. It was far too easy for people to hide behind data protection, Callie caught herself thinking angrily, before having to admit to herself that she was glad her personal details wouldn't just be handed over to any Tom, Dick or Harry conman.

Unsurprisingly, she found that the smaller one-man firms were easier to get information from, as the person answering the phone was usually the driver him or herself or their wife/husband, but the first two were unable to help in that they were categorically able to tell her that they hadn't been booked for Mrs Mount's trip. Refusing to give up, Callie rang the third on her list.

"Hello, dear, do you need a taxi?" a woman asked and Callie wondered why else she thought someone would ring a taxi firm.

"Er, not just at the moment."

"So, how can I help you? When do you need the booking for? Just a moment while I get the diary." There was a rustling noise as the woman opened a paper planner; no computers at this firm. "Fire away, I'm ready."

Callie crossed her fingers that this woman was going to be as helpful as she seemed.

"I don't actually want to make a booking," Callie told her, "I just want some information, if that's possible? My name is Dr Hughes and I work with the police." Callie went through the same spiel as she had with all the other firms. "So, can you tell me if you had a call to a Mrs Mount on the first? The journey was from St Peter's Road to the station."

There was a bit of rustling as the woman found the right page in the diary.

"Um, no. I'm sorry, dear." The lady sounded genuinely sad not to be of any use.

"No, you can't help or no, you didn't have that booking?" Callie queried.

"No, we didn't have that one. Nothing for a Mrs Mount. No bookings at all that day, if I'm honest. My husband doesn't get a lot of work now, he just does a bit to help people out, that sort of thing. Can I ask why you're asking? Nothing wrong, I hope?"

There was no disguising the curiosity in her question. She was clearly desperate to know why the police were checking who had taken the booking and Callie couldn't blame her: it was probably the most interesting thing to happen to her all week.

"It's nothing important," Callie said cheerfully. "Mrs Mount was unable to go that day because she had sadly died, and the family wanted to compensate the driver who came out," she lied. If she did get hold of the driver though, it would be worth her while to pay him just to have got the information.

"That's nice," the woman said. "Not that the old lady died," she hastily corrected herself, "but that the family want to make the payment anyway. Not many people would be that considerate. You wouldn't believe the number of people who book a taxi and then forget to cancel it when they change their minds. They seem to think that just because you haven't actually done the journey, you aren't losing anything. But there's the time, and getting to the pick-up location. It all costs."

"Absolutely. Well, thank you for answering my question." Callie cut her off quickly before she went into a full-on rant. It was disappointing to be crossing the firm off her list; she had been so hopeful at the beginning of their conversation.

"I mean, it wasn't your lady, but we had a similar one up at the mobile home park."

"Oh, yes?" Callie was suddenly interested again.

"I just say this because you mentioned the call was to the station."

"When was this?"

"Hmm, I'll have to look back and see." More rustling. "Now what was her name. Something, Ethel? No, it was a flower or a month or something. Rose? May?"

"June?" Callie couldn't help herself.

"June! That's right, dear. I said it was strange to be getting a booking for a June in June," she laughed. "June Dingwell. I remember now because I thought she said Dingle, you know, like the family in Emmerdale, but she spelled it out. D I N G W E L L." She gave Callie each letter, just as, presumably, June Dingwell had when she booked the taxi.

"What date was that?"

"I'm just looking back through the book, dear. It was quite a while ago." More rustling. "Here we are. The third of last month, I remember the call now."

"Is she a regular of yours?"

"No, no, never been to her before as far as I know."

"And she asked to go to the bus station?"

"That's right."

"Did she say why?"

"Who? The young lady that booked it? No, not that I remember, she just wanted a taxi there for 10 a.m. To take her to the station. But when Dick, my husband – he does the driving you see – got there, there was no answer. We found out later she'd died. So sad."

"It wasn't Mrs Dingwell herself who made the booking?"

"No, now, let me think, I'm sure she said she was her niece. Does that make sense?"

Callie gave it some thought. There was certainly a niece in Mrs Dingwell's case. Eleanor had mentioned that Dr Richardson was worried about some sort of comeback from a niece, which was why he hadn't wanted her to speak to Callie.

"Yes, that does make sense. Thank you so much for your help," Callie said. "Please call me if you remember anything else." And she gave the woman her number.

"Not at all, dear – you just ring me up if you need anything more, and if Mrs Dingwell's family want to compensate us for the journey, it would be much appreciated. I can't say as I'll hold my breath though – people like that are few and far between."

Once she had put down the phone, Callie sat thinking about the call. In some ways, she was disappointed. If different taxi firms had been used, they couldn't be the link, and the fact that the niece had booked the taxi made it more likely that this was a genuine case of someone who had simply died the day she was due to go away. Callie made a note to ask Eleanor if she knew anything more about the niece.

# Chapter 13

Next morning, Callie was sitting in the main doctor's office, supposedly doing administration. The pile of letters and prescription requests in her basket was deceptively low, as most admin work came electronically these days, but even so, she wasn't really tackling it. She was in fact going through the information she had been emailed from Eleanor, Angus and Caroline.

In Eleanor's case, it was pretty sparse. Unsurprisingly, she clearly didn't want to run any risks around patient confidentiality. Callie had managed to speak to her that morning and told her about June Dingwell's niece having booked the taxi.

"Gosh, that is a relief," she had said, sounding surprised. "So she probably isn't connected to your lady?"

"Possibly not, but I wondered if I could have her details – the niece, that is – so that I can just check."

There were a few moments of silence.

"Er, I don't know." Eleanor was clearly not keen.

"Or you could ring her," Callie suggested. "Just so we can definitely cross her off the list."

"Okay, yes. I'll do that," Eleanor answered brightly. "And just to let you know, my transfer to Dr Grantham has been agreed, and I'm starting with you on Monday."

"Great! I'll look forward to seeing you." Callie had mixed feelings; on the one hand she was pleased to have helped the bullied trainee but on the other hand, if she turned out to be a liability Hugh Grantham would never let Callie forget it. She would be scheduled to do the baby clinics every week for eternity.

Callie had found a great deal more information in both Caroline's and Angus's emailed responses. They had each sent a copy of all their patient notes for the two deaths and also written an account of what they remembered of the scene.

Alan Darling had been found dead on the seventeenth of June. Callie started a timeline, beginning with June Dingwell on the third, who would remain on her list until she could definitively be removed; Alan Darling on the seventeenth; and Elizabeth Mount on the first of July. Callie paused. Each death was exactly two weeks apart. On a Tuesday. Of course, people died every day, but that such similar deaths should have occurred at such precise intervals was strange. What were the odds? It certainly added to the probability that she was right to keep June Dingwell on the list, at least until it could be confirmed whether or not her holiday plans were genuine.

Callie went through the notes on Alan Darling and Elizabeth Mount. Both had lived alone and neither had relatives – at least, none known by their doctors. Both had suffered from mild dementia and were receiving care packages from social services and also had regular visits from the community nursing team. All three had been found dead, sitting in a chair, waiting to go on holiday. There was no mention of any bruising indicating recent blood samples having been taken in either of the first two deaths, but if they were wearing long sleeves, no one would have checked that. Why would they? Neither of the first two cases had been completely unexpected and they had been seen recently, so their own doctors had been willing to sign the death certificates. That meant that there was no call for post-mortems or coroner involvement.

Both deaths were deemed to be due to natural causes. It was only because Caroline had told her husband about finding Mr Darling, apparently ready to go on holiday, that Angus had called Callie when Mrs Mount appeared to be prepared to do the same. That, and the fact that he hadn't seen Mrs Mount in the last few weeks and so it had to be a coroner's case. In circumstances like these, Callie knew, any post-mortem and inquest would have been fairly perfunctory. Old people die, and there was no obvious cause of death that would ring any alarms. A more thorough investigation had been carried out in Mrs Mount's case, but purely because Angus had called Callie in and she had then alerted Billy. That and the fact that Billy was more thorough than most people anyway; it was one of the things she loved about him. One of the many things. And his findings had shown that both chloride and potassium levels were far enough above normal to raise his suspicions – to the point where he had actually called it murder. So it was her fault that he was in this position. She just had to find the evidence to back him up. Unfortunately, she could find nothing more in any of the information sent by her colleagues that helped her at all.

And then Eleanor rang back to say that she had spoken to Mrs Dingwell's niece, and she had said her aunt had been coming to stay with her.

Callie scratched through her name on the timeline, crossly. She didn't wish ill on the old lady, but being back down to only two suspicious deaths made her task of proving some kind of misconduct had occurred that much more difficult.

With a sigh of defeat, Callie put down her timeline and concentrated on her day job, her proper job, as her mother liked to call it, refusing to acknowledge that being a police doctor was anything more than a rather macabre hobby, like taxidermy or collecting death masks.

She was finding it hard to concentrate on the letters about haemorrhoids and hip operations and her mind kept drifting off to Billy and what she could do to help him. She was reading a note about one of her patients, from the community nursing team, and the second time she read it, trying to take in what it said, she noticed that it was signed by a Trudy Wells. Trudy – of course! – she thought. That was the name of the nurse who had been at Mrs Mount's home and found her dead.

Callie fished out the list of questions she had written down to try and help her think of a way forward. The day job could wait.

Question one had been about the community nurses, question two about charities or social services arranging holidays. Question three about taxi firms and question four, the big one: why?

She had no idea where to start with question four.

Question three she had thought was answered, because Mrs Mount and Mrs Dingwell used different firms, but if Mrs Dingwell was scratched off the list, she was back to square one. She would have to call round again and try to find out if a taxi had been booked for Alan Darling, and if so, which one.

She'd marginally narrowed down question two after talking to Helen Austen as she had been able to cross off social services as the people organising the holidays, if they were real, but hadn't successfully contacted any churches or charities yet. Not much progress there, then.

And she hadn't even made a start on question one, she realised. The community nurse team. Maybe now was the time. Both Alan Darling and Mrs Mount were definitely on their visit list. How could she find out who had been visiting them both? Callie knew it almost certainly wouldn't be just one person. There were a lot of nurses covering Hastings and they worked in teams attached to surgeries, or was it by area? Callie didn't know, never having really paid much attention; she just knew that they worked in small teams to try and reduce the number of different people seeing any individual patient. She also knew it didn't really work, because patients often complained they didn't see the same person twice. Of course, when one of the team was a bit rough or unpleasant, or didn't understand the way they liked things to be done, seeing somebody different could be a bonus.

Callie looked at the note she had received from Trudy Wells, which was a request for a prescription of antibiotics for Mrs Stanhope. No details of why she needed them, which really irritated Callie. She never liked to write a prescription for a broad-spectrum antibiotic without knowing what it was for. Given Mrs Stanhope's history it was likely that her leg ulcer was infected again, but it hadn't looked that way when she visited; if it had, Callie would have sent off a swab while she was there. She always preferred to do that so that she could make sure that the antibiotic was the right one. She checked to see if one had been sent by Trudy or any other nurse but there was no mention of a swab having been taken by her or anyone else. It was as good an excuse to get hold of Trudy as any. She reached for the telephone.

"Hi, Trudy," she said when the answerphone kicked in. "It's Dr Hughes here. I wonder if I can have a word about one of my patients you've been seeing, a Mrs Stanhope? You've asked for antibiotics for her. Could you give me a call when you get this message? Thank you."

She left her number and wondered if she was likely to get a call back. Experience suggested that Trudy was not the sort of nurse who was reliable when it came to communicating with GPs, but at least she'd taken the first step. If she didn't get a reply that morning, she would have a very good reason to contact her manager.

While she waited in vain for a call back, Callie googled charities for dementia sufferers and the elderly. She sent email questions to all the large ones, asking if they organised holidays for elderly patients with mild dementia. She also made a note of the smaller, more local, charities that were concerned with people and families of dementia sufferers. There were two with offices in town, so she thought she might go in and call on them personally.

Much as she tried to turn her attention back to her paperwork while she waited for the nurse to call her back, Callie couldn't keep her mind on it. Deciding some fresh air and an early lunch might be a good idea, she grabbed her bag and headed out. It would give her a chance to drop into the two local charities as well, she told herself. The paperwork could wait; she could always come in over the weekend to catch up.

\* \* \*

Walking down the road between the shopping centre and the bus station where the first of the charities was based, Callie rehearsed what she was going to say. She intended to use her mother just as she had told Kate, but hoped she didn't have to give any contact details – at least, not before she had had a chance to warn her mother. Callie could only imagine what she would say if some charity rang up suggesting she was getting a bit forgetful!

The first charity turned out to have closed down. Their shop, situated just behind the Priory shopping centre, was empty apart from a bunch of flyers and free papers on the mat and a note on the doorway giving the number of a property management service to call in emergencies.

Callie pressed on towards the railway station and the second address she had found.

This turned out to be a shop as well, and was also the head office for the Ada Holmes Charity, according to Callie's research. AHC, as it styled itself on the website, provided support, both psychological and physical, to the families of dementia sufferers. When she reached the address, Callie thought the charity could do with a bit of support itself. The shopfront looked in need of more than a bit of love and attention; it needed repainting, repointing and a jolly good clean, but at least it was still running.

In the window there was a jumble of donated objects, not arranged in any sort of display, but more as if everything had been shoved in there any old how. A while back Callie had watched a television programme where a marketing expert had shown a charity shop how to make their displays more attractive and encourage customers in. It had worked and the charity had doubled their income rapidly. This group could clearly do with watching the programme.

A bell jangled as she pushed open the door and Callie smiled at the woman who was standing behind the counter, closely watching a man who was rummaging through some jackets and coats. He looked as if he lived on the streets and he could certainly do with a new jacket; the one he had on was filthy. Like the woman behind the counter, Callie was sure he didn't intend to pay for a new one.

"Hello," Callie said to the middle-aged woman. "I wonder if there's someone I can talk to about my mother? Get some advice?"

She reluctantly turned to Callie, all the while trying to keep an eye on the possible shoplifter.

"Do you have an appointment?"

"Do I need one? Sorry. I just called in because, well, I'm desperate. Please?" Callie tried to look like someone at the end of their tether, but at that moment the shopper tried to slip a jacket under his baggy, dirty coat.

"Stop!" the woman shouted, and rushed towards the door in an effort to stop the man, but despite his old and decrepit appearance he could certainly put on a surprising turn of speed. He was out of the door and sprinting towards the shopping centre before she could stop him. Callie could only admire how fit he was; she didn't think she could run that fast.

"Really!" The woman complained as she returned to the till. "It's ridiculous. That's the second time this week we've had shoplifters. I mean, if he'd asked, I would probably have let him have it."

"He did look like he needed a new jacket."

"If you see him later, he won't be wearing it, I can guarantee it," the woman said, dismissively. "He'll have swapped it for a can of strong cider."

Callie knew she was probably right. People often thought they were helping when they gave street beggars food or coats rather than money which they rightly thought would be spent on drugs or alcohol, but often these items were just sold on to feed their real need, their addiction.

The woman picked up the phone by the till and Callie wondered if she was calling the police, but it seemed she was calling the office upstairs.

"Joyce? We've just had another one, stole a ski jacket this time, oh and there's a lady here needs to talk to someone, can I send her up?"

Callie was allowed behind the counter where there was a door, leading to a small hallway. Opening off from there, Callie could see that there was a kitchenette, a toilet, a room filled floor-to-ceiling with black plastic bags spilling assorted clothes, books and toys, and some stairs.

"Up here!" a friendly voice called as Callie started up the stairs.

The office at the top turned out to be a surprisingly tidy and well-organised space. It was cheaply but practically furnished and had several healthy plant specimens in pots along the windowsill. As someone whose fingers were definitely not green, Callie wondered what the secret was, but knew that whatever it was, she didn't have it. She would never be able to keep a plant alive longer than a week.

Seated at the desk was the woman behind the voice; her appearance didn't take away from the friendly impression.

She had long, curly, greying hair, partly held in place by an assortment of slides and combs, and she wore dangly earrings that didn't quite match the chunky necklace round her neck. Her clothes were an explosion of colour and patterns and styles that on anyone else would have jarred, but on her, they worked. She was colourful and bright and Callie immediately warmed to her.

"Come in, come in!" the woman said, indicating a chair opposite her, bangles jangling on her wrist as she did so. "I'm Joyce, now have a seat and tell me how I can help."

"It's my mother." Callie felt incredibly guilty as she started telling this kind and caring woman a string of lies about having to care for her mother with dementia while having to work full time, and now needing to go into hospital for an operation.

"Does she have carers coming in?" Joyce asked.

"Yes, and they do a great job, even if they can only be there for twenty minutes each visit."

"It's hard for them to do anything meaningful in twenty minutes, isn't it?"

"Yes," Callie sighed.

She knew Joyce was right. It was something people often complained to her about. Twenty minutes was not enough time to bathe someone, or sit and chat to them, and company was sometimes the thing they needed most. The carers rushed in, got their patient up and dressed, gave them any medication they needed and left, having flung a cup of tea or a piece of toast in front of them. They had no time to do any more. But equally, she understood the economics of it. If they stayed longer, they would help fewer patients, and then the money the care organisation was paid wouldn't cover their wages. There was never enough money, so there was never enough time.

"Do you live with your mother?" Joyce was busy making notes.

"No, I have, other commitments." Callie was desperate not to have to go into that. "I call in after work. Do the things the carers don't have time to do. Put her to bed, make sure she's okay. You know?"

Joyce smiled.

"We could see about a volunteer to come and sit with her, do what you normally do. It could only be short term—"

"Really?" Callie made a mental note to remember this charity; that would be a great help to some of her patients, to get them through shortfalls in care when their normal carer was away. Much better than respite care. "I worry that if she stays home, she'll expect me to be there, wonder where I am, even if I've told her a million times."

"You're thinking of respite care?" Joyce looked sad. "To be honest, it's very hard to come by."

"Oh, I wondered if maybe you sometimes organised it, or a holiday for them. I mean, Mum's not bad, she's just a bit forgetful, worries a lot."

"We don't have the resources for that sort of solution, unfortunately," Joyce said regretfully. "Much as we would like to. All we have are a few volunteers – all vetted, of course," she hastily reassured Callie, "people who are experienced with the elderly and can offer to keep them company, do practical tasks like shopping or changing a light bulb, that sort of thing."

"That sounds really helpful." Callie was definitely going to have to remember the Ada Holmes Charity; that sort of support was exactly what so many of her patients needed. "Do you have a lot of volunteers?"

"Not as many as we need," Joyce said. "Now if you would like to give me your details?"

Callie decided it was time to beat a hasty retreat, so she gave her phone number, the dates she would supposedly be in hospital and, after a moment's hesitation, Kate's address as that of her mother and stood up.

"I'll speak to my mother and make sure she's happy and then get back to you, shall I? To confirm things?"

"That will be fine. Once we have a volunteer sorted, they will need to come and visit your mother, with you there, just to introduce them to her and make sure everyone is happy."

"Great. That sounds a very sensible thing to do. I can't tell you how much you've put my mind at rest, Joyce."

Joyce stood as well and held out her hand.

"It was lovely to meet you, Miss Hughes, and don't forget, we are not just there for the elderly, we are here for the whole family. Carers like you need support too, so if you ever need to talk to someone, you know where we are now."

And Callie left the office feeling even more of a heel than she had before.

# Chapter 14

"Honestly, Kate, I felt awful. She was such a nice person. You would have loved her style, all bright colours and big jewellery."

They were in The Stag, sitting outside in the small but pretty garden, basking in the last of the sunshine. Billy would have joined them but he had decided to visit his parents and break the news that there was a question mark over his planned move to Belfast. Callie had no idea what they would say, but she hoped they would be supportive and able to help with his disappointment. She knew his mum would ask him to join her in her GP practice in South London, because she always did, and he always refused, saying he preferred his patients dead, but maybe this time, under these circumstances, he would be tempted. She was sure it would be the wrong move for him and hoped he stayed strong.

"They don't arrange holidays though, you said?"

"Officially no, but when I thought about it, I wondered if one of their volunteers could tell the old people that they do, that they can arrange one. I mean, I realised, as I was talking to Joyce, the woman there, that the holidays don't actually have to be real, in fact they can't be because they aren't going to go, and the killer knows that."

"Very true. If they were real holidays that had been arranged with a hotel or whatever, people would be wondering why they hadn't turned up."

"Exactly."

Kate frowned as she took a handful of crisps.

"That would mean that it's all been planned. He, or she, knew that they were going to kill them from the very start."

Callie nodded.

"Yes. I know. Awful as that is, I can't really get any other explanation to fit."

"It's so cold-blooded. Surely there must be another explanation?"

"I can't find one," Callie replied. "There isn't anywhere that legitimately arranges holidays for the elderly and confused. The only option is respite care in residential care homes, or home, as there's only one place that does it round here. And, before you ask, I checked – none of the victims were due to go there, or even on a waiting list for a place."

"How did you manage to get that information?" Kate raised an eyebrow.

"There are some advantages to being a doctor, you know. I was merely making enquiries about some of my patients."

Kate took a hefty swig of beer, and the last of the crisps, and looked thoughtful.

"Well, if that really is what's going on, we need to stop it."

"Agreed."

"What we need is a list of clients supported by the charity and also their volunteers, so we can check out how many of the former have died, and how many of the latter are serial killers."

Callie looked anxiously round, she didn't want anyone overhearing this conversation and getting the wrong idea. Or even the right idea.

"I know, but, joking aside, I don't know how we are going to get that information."

"And these deaths have been occurring every two weeks?"

"Well, the two we are sure about, they were two weeks apart."

"Yes, it's a shame you've had to lose the first death," Kate hesitated. "I can't believe I just said that, if you know what I mean?"

"Yes, I do." Callie nodded. "Completely. It was just so neat. I got Mike Parton to check the register to see if anyone else suitable died the same day as June Dingwell, or on any Wednesday before, but he couldn't find any sudden deaths, well, none that could easily fit with our other two."

"If it's only just started, that's good, but if it is a two-week gap, then−"

"The next one is due to happen this Tuesday," Callie confirmed.

"Which doesn't give us much time to find out who is doing this."

"Exactly. Which is why I have a plan. Well, two plans, actually."

"What makes me think I'm not going to like them?" Kate asked.

"Well, one of them is not a problem for you. I'm going to follow up on the nurse I told you about. Find out about her other client lists. Just because the murderous charity volunteer idea fits so nicely, I don't want to lose sight of other possibilities."

"Okay and how are you going to do that?"

"I'm going to make an official complaint about her."

"That's a bit harsh, isn't it?"

"I do have legitimate grounds," Callie insisted. "She never got back to me about a patient she requested antibiotics for, and that really isn't good enough. I had to go round and take a swab and check on the patient before I could do a prescription. Even if this wasn't going on, I would be tempted to raise it with her manager."

"Okay, I can see she's irritated you," Kate agreed. "And you think you will be able to find out more from her manager?"

"Exactly. I'll be able to dig a bit, I hope."

"And the second plan?"

"Ah, yes, well... that involves you and my mother."

Kate raised an eyebrow.

"I really can't wait to hear this one."

* * *

If Callie had thought for a moment that it would be difficult to persuade her mother to go along with her plan, she was wrong. It turned out that Diana was very happy to help. In fact, she was very enthusiastic about it.

"I will have such an exciting story to tell everyone at bridge club, darling."

"I'll be there the whole time," Callie had reassured her father, seeing as her mother didn't seem to need the reassurance.

"I'm sure your mother is quite capable of looking after herself," he had replied. "And you don't expect anything to happen at this meeting, do you?"

"Absolutely not," Callie had responded. "I'm just going to see if I get any response to my request for Mummy to have a holiday."

"Seems a bit of a long shot."

And she knew he was right, as always. But she didn't have any other ideas. So, she had set up a visit from the volunteer who had been allocated to them, for him to get to know her mother. The visit was set for early Monday evening, at Kate's house, as that was where she had said her mother lived. Callie just hoped that both she and Diana were up to maintaining the subterfuge.

Working on the other strand of her investigation, first thing Monday morning, having made sure that Eleanor had arrived and was settled and had been introduced to all the staff who were in, Callie checked to see if she had had a response from Trudy Wells. There was none, so she went to her own consulting room, wanting some privacy for what she was about to do next. She telephoned the community nurse team to make a formal complaint against the nurse and requested a meeting with her manager later that day. She was still waiting for a reply several hours later when she decided to call it a day. It seemed that both manager and nurse had similar response times.

Which all explained why she found herself sitting in Kate's living room, with her mother tucked up in a chair with a rug over her knees, waiting for the volunteer from the Ada Holmes Charity to arrive and meet them.

"There's a flaw in your plan, you know, darling," Diana said once Callie had got her settled.

"Oh?" Callie replied. "What's that?"

"No one is going to seriously believe that this house is decorated to my taste." And she looked meaningfully round the living room, with its velvet curtains, ethnic throws and large number of cushions in a variety of colours. Callie knew that she had a point. A quick whizz around the room, removing most of the offending articles, helped but left Callie feeling a little sad; it was no longer the friendly, homely place she identified with her friend and had grown to love. Needs must, she told herself. It still wasn't perfect for an old lady's home, but it wasn't bad.

Kate had been happy to let them borrow her home for an evening for this part of the plan. She had laughed at the thought of Callie's mum pretending to have Alzheimer's and had taken herself off to the gym, still giggling. Callie knew that her friend frequented the leisure centre, not to exercise, but to see if she could find a good-looking young man who might want to take her out for a drink, which she usually did, so she wasn't expecting Kate back any time soon.

"That smell?" Diana said, sniffing the air. "Is it—?"

"Just potpourri, Mummy." Callie had also recognised the faint whiff of spliff as they sat waiting for their visitor, but she didn't want to say as much to her mother. "Or an air freshener."

"Hmm, wouldn't have put Kate down as the sort of girl to use either. Let's hope our charity worker can't recognise the smell of cannabis."

Just when Callie was beginning to have second thoughts about her plan, the doorbell rang. This was it.

# Chapter 15

"Would you like some more tea, Mr, er, what did you say your name was?" Diana waved at the visitor in a vague manner. Callie hoped she wasn't going to overdo the frail old dear act.

"No, no, thank you, Mrs Hughes, and it's Parsons, Derek Parsons, but you can call me Derek, if you like."

"That's very kind, Derek, and, in that case, you can call me Diana."

Callie raised her eyebrows; it was very unlike her mother to get on first name terms with anyone so quickly. It was true that Derek exuded a quiet and caring air that invited you to be on easy terms, but still.

"Are you quite sure?" he asked her. "I wouldn't want to presume if you prefer to be called Mrs Hughes."

"I'm very sure, Derek. But thank you for checking. No one else does. It's Diana this, Diana that from the nurses, and only the other day one of them referred to me as Di!"

"Oh, dear." Derek tutted and shook his head at this breach of protocol.

"I'll have a word with them, Mummy," Callie said, only for her mother to ignore her completely.

"You have a lovely home, Mrs— Diana," Derek said, correcting himself.

"Hmph," Diana responded. "It could do with a good clean, but I don't seem to have the energy these days."

"Don't you worry about it. It's perfectly fine," Derek reassured her. "I may be able to help you with a few bits of cleaning when I come and visit. That's if you would like me to come and visit?"

"That would be so nice of you, Derek. My daughter," she glared accusingly at Callie, "hardly ever comes to see me. She hasn't been here in weeks, you know."

"Mummy! That just isn't true!" Callie exclaimed. "I come round every day after work. It's just that she forgets," she explained to Derek, who nodded.

"Of course, of course, I quite understand."

"And now she's leaving me to go on holiday," Diana continued.

"Into hospital, Mummy," Callie corrected her and turned to Derek. "I'm sorry about this. She doesn't seem to understand."

"I understand perfectly well, I just don't believe you," Diana retorted. "You are always off gallivanting with your men friends. Leaving me to look after myself."

Callie opened her mouth but couldn't quite think of how to respond to this accusation, even if it was just her mother play-acting. She was doing it a little too well and enjoying it too much for Callie's liking. She was left wondering if her mother really was having a dig at her for not visiting enough. It had been a while since she had been to see her parents, she had to admit. To cover her discomfort, she grabbed the tray of tea things and went into the kitchen. Derek followed with his own mug.

"It's all right," Derek said to her quietly. "I understand exactly what you're going through. I looked after my own mother for many years and she was always accusing me of not visiting, of abandoning her or even of hiding things from her."

"I find it so hard that she always blames me."

"Yes, so you mustn't blame yourself, it only makes things worse. I see it all the time. Now do you have any questions?"

He seemed so nice that Callie really couldn't picture him as a killer, but then, she'd been wrong about that sort of thing in the past.

"Are there many people like you?" she asked him. "Visiting the elderly?"

"About six at the moment," he answered. "I'm the only man, though. Is that a problem?"

"No, no, I don't think so," she reassured him. "It's just that I met another lady, a Jean something," Callie paused, trying to remember the name of the neighbour she had met at Mrs Mount's.

"Lovejoy," Derek helpfully filled in for her.

"You know her?" Callie didn't have to fake surprise, she hadn't known that Jean Lovejoy was with the charity until that moment. "She used to help a friend of mine."

"Oh, well you might be able to get Jean if you would prefer a woman. I know she's free, but you would have to speak to Joyce."

He seemed really disappointed that she might have someone else in mind for her mother.

"No honestly, my mother seems to have taken a shine to you."

He beamed with pleasure at this.

"Are all the visitors people who have experience looking after partners with dementia?"

"Partners or parents. It really helps, you know."

"Of course, I understand, and do you have many people that you visit? Clients?" she asked.

"We all only have one person to visit at any time," Derek said. "It's important to build up a relationship with them and be free to come when they need you to. You can't just send someone else if you are busy elsewhere."

"I can imagine. So, you haven't got a client at the moment?"

"No, my last, well, lovely old man that he was, he died a couple of weeks ago."

"Ah, I'm sorry."

"Yes, it is hard when they pass. I had got quite attached to him and it was like losing Mum, all over again."

He seemed genuinely moved which made it hard for Callie to probe further. She really wanted to find out the man's name, or at least something that would indicate whether or not it was Mr Darling but she couldn't think how. Then she spotted something on the kitchen table. Kate had left a pile of work folders on the kitchen table with the name of her legal practice printed on the front.

"I'm so relieved you understand." Callie quickly took the mug off Derek and put it in the sink. "I feel I can trust you to care for my mother. Now—" She wanted to get him out of the kitchen before he saw them, but when she turned back, she saw that Derek was already looking at them.

"Do you work at a legal practice then?" he asked. "Only we are always needing legal help with doing things like sorting out powers of attorney and wills. Things like that."

"Really?" Callie ushered him out of the room before he spotted the photo of a naked man stuck to the fridge door as well.

"Yes, we do our best to help wherever we can," Derek continued as they went back into the living room. "Of course, we don't have much money." He looked meaningfully at her.

"I understand that. I'll talk to Joyce," she said. "See if we can get something sorted out."

Derek beamed and turned to Diana.

"Now are we happy to continue with my visits, Diana, while your daughter is in hospital?"

"What we really need, or rather I need, is to go on holiday too," Diana replied.

"Mummy, I've already explained, I'm—"

"Oh, I don't want to go away with you." Diana continued waving a hand dismissively at Callie. "I want to go somewhere with a nice hotel. Somewhere where they know how to look after the older generation. Perhaps like the place we used to go when your father was still with us." She seemed to drift away for a moment. "You know, somewhere like Torquay."

If Callie didn't know that her father was safely at home with his whisky and the crossword and that, as far as she knew, they had never had a holiday in Torquay, she would have been taken in. Her mother's performance was pitch perfect.

"Now, Diana," Derek patted her hand, "don't you go upsetting yourself. We can talk about holidays at a later point, but we don't organise them at the charity. We can't. Your daughter would have to do that, but I can advise her on some lovely places to stay." He looked at Callie. "Places that accommodate the older client."

"Thank you so much, Donald, is it? Or—?"

"Derek, Derek Parsons."

"Yes, of course. I'm so sorry, sometimes I forget."

"It's not a problem. I promise. You can call me by any name you want."

"A rose by any other name."

Derek smiled and patted Diana's hand and she smiled at him. Callie inwardly groaned. Her mother was actually flirting with him.

"It's so nice to be visited by someone who actually cares," Diana continued and looked pointedly at Callie, who felt a little sick.

"I'll show you out, Mr Parsons," she said, standing up.

Derek stood up as well.

"And you must call me Derek, too," he said as he walked towards the door. "Your mother will find it less confusing."

"Of course." Callie opened the door. "What happens next?" she asked him.

"You need to contact Joyce and agree what days you'd like me to visit. There's some paperwork that needs to be done, and a contract and that, but you must be used to that sort of thing."

It took a moment or two before she remembered that Derek thought she worked at a law firm.

"Of course."

"I'll get off now and let you two talk." He turned to Callie's mother and called out, "Goodbye, Diana, and thank you for the tea."

"Goodbye, er, young man. I do hope you come again soon."

Callie quickly saw him out before her mother said something really embarrassing.

If Callie thought that once Derek had gone she would be able to pack her mother off home straight away, she was sadly mistaken. Like any actress who has just put in a bravura performance, Diana wanted to relive it again, and again.

"Honestly, darling, he was completely taken in, he really thought I was a confused old woman."

There were a lot of comments Callie could have made to this, but wisely, she didn't.

"Would you like more tea?" she asked instead.

"Tea? I think a celebratory G & T is in order – that's if you haven't got any champagne."

Callie was pretty sure Kate would have some champagne somewhere, but she wasn't about to raid her friend's wine cellar. Instead she found a bottle of gin and some tonic in the fridge and poured her mother a drink. Just a small one; after all, she had to drive home, at least Callie hoped she was going to. She really didn't want her mother deciding to stay the night, even though she had been a great help. She handed the drink to her mother.

"No lemon, I'm afraid."

"I didn't expect it. Not here."

Callie looked as if she was about to jump in and defend her friend, but Diana held up a hand to stop her.

"No, you are right," she said. "Never criticise a person's housekeeping skills when you're drinking their gin."

After a few more reruns of the evening, the gin was finished and, much to Callie's relief, Diana decided it was time to go home and, no doubt, regale her husband with tales of how well it had gone.

"Honestly, Kate," Callie told her friend when she arrived back, mercifully alone, a few minutes after Callie had sent her a text message to let her know the coast was clear. "Anyone would think she was in line for an Oscar."

Kate laughed.

"I can imagine her loving every minute, but you should be grateful, she got some more information for you."

"Yes, I now know that Mrs Mount's visitor was from the charity and that it's likely Derek was visiting Mr Darling, from what he said."

"So that gives you a probable link to the charity."

"Yes, but it's still not as much as I was hoping for." Callie couldn't keep the disappointment from her voice. "I mean, two different visitors being involved? That seems pretty unlikely."

"True, but there's more. You said he was asking about power of attorney work?"

"Yes, he saw your files on the kitchen table and assumed I worked for the firm." Callie had a sudden idea. "Would you be able to find out if the charity or any of the volunteers benefited from the wills or anything?"

"Not so soon after the deaths," Kate replied, disappointingly. "Probate won't have been granted, so the contents of the wills won't be public knowledge. But, you know, that might well be a motive."

"Inheriting their money, you mean?" Callie was excited by this idea.

"That or holding power of attorney and then emptying their accounts."

"It would be a great motive," Callie agreed, excitedly. "I hadn't thought of that. How can we find out?"

"Well, maybe my new clerk can offer my services, free of charge, to the charity."

"Your new clerk?"

"That's you."

"Oh, yes, of course. You know, that's a really great idea, Kate."

Kate looked smug.

"It won't necessarily get me a look at any power of attorney or wills from before, but at least we might get to know how they operate moving forward."

"Brilliant. And thank you."

"Not at all, if they are crooked, I want to stop them and if they aren't, well, I'm happy to help."

"I'll let Joyce know tomorrow," Callie said, picking up her bag and preparing to go home. "When I tell her that my operation's been cancelled so we won't be needing Derek's services after all."

# Chapter 16

At lunchtime the next day, when Callie went upstairs to complete her paperwork after her morning surgery, she found a note to tell her that the manager of the community care team had called and would be in his office at lunchtime if she wanted to speak to him.

Checking her visit list, she could see that she had a patient to see quite near to where the offices were, so she decided to go and see him in person.

The community nursing team worked out of an office building they shared with the social services care team. The theory was that the two services would have better communication if they cohabited a building, as they so often shared clients, but Callie wasn't sure it worked. The building itself had seen better days, to put it mildly. The car park had more potholes than tarmac, which couldn't be good for the tyres on the fleet of small cars that the carers used.

Callie found a space between two white cars with the words "Hastings Care" in green lettering on the side, along with the company logo.

There was no one on the reception desk when she went in, but she made a quick call to the manager and he hurried out to meet her and take her through to his office.

"Dr Hughes! Welcome!" He smoothed his hair nervously – or rather, he smoothed what was left of his gelled spikes. Despite probably only being in his thirties, his hairline had receded alarmingly.

He didn't introduce himself, and there was no clue on his office door, so Callie belatedly stuck out her hand.

"Please, call me Callie," she said and waited expectantly.

"Er, John," he admitted reluctantly, shaking her outstretched hand. "John Turner, manager of the community team. Please come in."

Pleased to have at least extracted his name, Callie entered his office and took a seat.

"I understand that you want to make a complaint against Trudy Wells, Dr Hughes?" the manager said once they were safely in his office, with the door closed. "You could have just telephoned, you know? Or emailed again?"

"Yes, but I always find it better to do things in person," she told him.

The manager clearly didn't agree and he tidied the already immaculate files on his desk.

"As I explained before," Callie continued, "she has failed to respond to my request for information, and this isn't the first instance."

"No, well, the team's very busy at the moment," Turner said nervously. "She probably hasn't had the time."

"But it's just not good enough. It causes more work for everyone else, because they have to do things she should have done, and may well have done, but how can we know? And, what's more I have heard from some of my patients that she hasn't turned up when she is supposed to or that her manner is, well, quite frankly, rude."

The manager cleared his throat, adjusted his tie and smoothed his hair again. He really wasn't happy.

"Do you have specific instances? I mean, if I am to start any kind of proceedings against her, I will need proof that there is a problem. I can't just go accusing her of things without any evidence."

Callie had expected Turner to be defensive and it seemed she was right to have done so. She told him about Mrs Stanhope with her leg ulcer and the swab she had to go and do because Nurse Wells hadn't.

"She was also really quite rude to both me and Dr McPhail when we were at the house of a deceased patient of his, Mrs Mount, and I did hear, although you would have to confirm it, there was a problem when she visited Mr Darling, one of Dr Stratton's patients."

That was a little white lie, and she hoped she was right that he was unlikely to call Caroline or Angus – indeed, that he was unlikely to even consider them in the context of her complaint. All Callie was hoping for was some sort of confirmation that Nurse Wells had visited Mr Darling too, but there was no reaction at all. Although, Callie had to admit even to herself that the fact that the manager didn't bat an eyelid might mean that Mr Darling was also on Nurse Wells's visit list, or that he hadn't a clue who did what to whom in his organisation.

"Perhaps we could ask Nurse Wells about these incidents?" she suggested. "And about a Mrs Dingwell and Harry Hunt." Callie had just made the name up to see if there was any different reaction at all. There wasn't. So, the manager didn't know who was on anyone's visit list.

"Erm, she's not here at the moment." The manager adjusted his tie again. "In fact, she's off sick, so I can't put your complaints to her, but I promise you, Dr Hughes, I will talk to her about it when she comes back."

"About all those patients?"

"Of course."

Callie didn't believe it for one moment. He hadn't even written down the names, although perhaps that was a good thing, as she didn't even know whether the nurse had visited two of them, and one of them was fictional.

"I will want to know the outcome of that conversation and any disciplinary action taken."

"Of course, Dr Hughes. I'll keep you fully informed." The manager stood abruptly and went to the office door. "Now, if you wouldn't mind, I'm really very busy."

Callie was being dismissed and there was little she could do about it, except wonder about why he was so agitated about their meeting.

As she carefully manoeuvred her car out of the car park, she wondered if perhaps he knew something really bad had happened and was trying to cover it up because he didn't want to lose his job. By really bad, of course, she meant something like a nurse in his employ going round killing his clients. That would be enough to make any manager a little jumpy, wouldn't it?

* * *

That afternoon it was baby clinic, a job that Callie dreaded, not because she didn't like babies. It was just that all that anxiety from the new mums and noise from the babies when they objected to being pulled about, weighed, measured and then, final insult, vaccinated, meant that it wasn't a restful couple of hours. She always seemed to end up with a headache.

The clinic was based in the waiting room, with the scales in one corner, a screened area for breastfeeding and a table laden with advice leaflets and free samples. Any babies or mothers who needed to be seen by a doctor were brought through to the consulting room once the health visitor had finished with them.

"Have you sat in on one of these before?" Callie asked Eleanor as they went into her room.

"Oh, yes, I did a couple when I was with Dr Richardson."

"Great, well, you crack on, I'm here if you need me."

Callie happily handed the session over to the trainee and indicated that Eleanor should sit in the doctor's chair. Callie pulled up a chair in the corner and put her basket of paperwork down on the examination couch. She intended to try and use the time to catch up on admin, while being on hand to support Eleanor or answer any questions from her.

As the afternoon wore on, Callie was relieved to find that Eleanor really didn't need her. She knew what she was doing and went about it in a competent, caring way.

"Did you enjoy your time in paediatrics at the hospital?" Callie asked her in a brief break between babies.

"Yes," Eleanor replied, "and no. I loved the kids of course." To Callie's mind there was no of course about it – in her experience some of them were really not very nice. "I went back, thought I'd specialise and even did a couple of years or so, but I hated that they were so ill and in pain, and then, sometimes they die." Her face clouded as she remembered it. "It was hard, and I decided to change tack." Then she brightened. "It's much nicer in the community because the vast majority of the children you see are fit and healthy."

"You are going to be a great GP," Callie told her, and Eleanor smiled, and even blushed a little bit.

"Thank you," she said, as yet another baby was brought in for her.

* * *

All day Tuesday, Callie had been waiting anxiously to hear if there was another body. If the killer had kept to his or her usual routine, she would have expected the body to have been found by lunchtime at the latest. She had asked Mike Parton to let her know if there were any sudden deaths, and after her appeal to her colleagues at the LMC meeting, she hoped they would let her know of any bodies found, all dressed up to go on holiday.

Billy came over after work, and they sat waiting for the phone to ring.

"I can't ring Mike again, he'll go spare."

"No," Billy agreed. "I've rung him a few times myself today, too. And anyway, he'll be off duty by now, won't he?"

"Yes, but he's left word with the duty sergeant that he's to be called for any sudden deaths."

Callie's phone rang and she snatched it up.

"Yes? Oh, hi Kate, no, no news as yet."

Billy slumped back down, disappointed.

"Perhaps no one's found the body yet," he said. He had a point, but the others had been found within a few hours of their deaths. Maybe she had got it wrong and there was no pattern? Or maybe they had both got it wrong and there was no killer at all?

# Chapter 17

It was halfway through her Wednesday morning surgery that she got the call from Mike Parton.

"I'm at the home of a Mr Marek Bartosz, he lives just off Bohemia Road." He gave her the address details.

"You think it's another one?" she asked.

"Elderly male, lived alone, sitting in a chair in his Sunday best. No suitcase though."

"I will be there as quickly as I can."

* * *

As she walked from the spot where she had parked her car, Callie looked around her and assessed the street. The houses were part of a terrace and had doors opening directly onto the pavement, not unlike Mrs Mount's home, but her home had been neat and spotlessly clean, even on the outside. These houses didn't seem to have had any money spent on them in recent years. The windows were in urgent need of repainting or replacing and the once-white render was cracked and hanging off the walls in places. Callie knew that didn't mean the people living there were necessarily poor – she'd heard of people living like paupers when they had thousands of pounds in the bank –

but it suggested that Mr Bartosz might have been struggling in one way or another.

She knew exactly which house it was, because Parton was waiting for her at the front door.

"Are we going to treat it like a crime scene?" she asked.

"I think we have to," he said, although he didn't seem certain at all and Callie could sympathise: the coroner had already said that in the previous deaths there was no crime, the police weren't investigating, and Professor Wadsworth had said his piece as well. "I've called for forensics."

"Good," she told him. "I'll take a quick look and then we'll leave it to them." She went back to her car for her crime scene clothing and equipment. Parton had also donned his protective gear and was waiting so they could enter together.

"He's in the living room," Parton told her as they went into the narrow hallway. There was no carpet on the floor and there was a lot of dust and dirt on the bare floorboards. Both Parton and Callie walked to the side to preserve the many footprints that were down the middle.

"There's been a lot of traffic through here," Callie observed.

"The carers arrived mob-handed because apparently he can be a little, um, handy."

Callie smiled and nodded her understanding. She knew that behaviour that had been considered acceptable in this man's youth – patting women on the bottom, lewd comments and so on – was not okay now, but it was hard for the elderly to adjust, particularly if they had dementia. It wasn't uncommon for them to forget that times had changed and revert to how they had once behaved with impunity, only to find that it caused offence now. Or perhaps it had always caused offence but now people were more likely to complain.

There was only one armchair in the living room, situated close to the unlit gas fire, and Callie could immediately see an elderly man sitting in it. He was dressed in clothing that might have been his Sunday best, but it was still old, grubby and creased. There was a burn hole in the front of his cardigan next to a greasy mark of unknown origin, and his shoes were worn and hadn't been polished in a long time. Callie leaned in and checked for a non-existent pulse at the old man's neck. Like Mrs Mount, his skin was cool to her touch, even through her nitrile gloves, but it was not fully cold.

She looked around the room. There was a table by the window covered in newspaper rather than a cloth and a single dining chair was set next to it. Apart from a dust-covered sideboard and a rug that had seen better days, there was nothing else in the room.

"No suitcase," Callie said. "What made you call me?"

Parton looked a little embarrassed.

"I had a quick look round and there is a small suitcase in the cupboard under the stairs," he said sheepishly. "I didn't touch it, except to give it a nudge to see if it was full or empty and it seemed to be full."

Callie nodded. It might not be quite so obviously connected to the others, but it made sense that the killer might be making a belated effort to cover their tracks.

Much as she wanted to roll up the dead man's sleeve and check whether or not he had a bruise from an injection, Callie knew that she would compromise the crime scene if she so interfered to that extent, and there was absolutely no doubt in her mind now that this was a crime scene. Just before she stood back, something caught her eye and she gently eased back the cuff of the man's jacket. She had spotted the edge of what could be a bruise on the back of the man's hand and once the jacket was moved fully out of the way, she could see that it was, and central to the bruise there was a puncture mark. She pointed it out to Parton.

"Hello?" There was a call from the doorway and Callie and Parton backtracked to the front door, trying to keep to the same path they had used on the way in.

Once outside, they pulled off their protective gear and Callie left Parton to hand over to the crime scene team.

As she waited for him at her car, Callie saw a small car drive up and park nearby. A uniformed community nurse got out of the driver's seat and approached the house. It was with a mix of relief and disappointment that Callie saw that the nurse was not Trudy Wells, but a lovely young woman called Anne, whom she had met on a number of occasions.

"Hello, Anne."

"Dr Hughes," she responded. "What's going on? Is it Mr Bartosz?"

"I'm afraid so. Do you see him regularly?"

"No, I've seen him a couple of times, when I've had to cover, but not recently."

"Do you know if he has any relatives?"

The nurse hesitated.

"No idea. To be frank he's supposed to be Trudy's patient, but John, the manager, asked me to pop in and check him."

"Why?"

Anne fidgeted before finally deciding to tell Callie.

"We had a call from one of her other patients that she was due to see this morning to say Trudy hadn't come, so we split her patients between the team and I said I'd check if she'd been here."

"I was told by your manager that she was off sick."

"Really? Is that what John told you? Well, she isn't. Not officially." Anne was clearly cross that she was having to cover for Trudy.

"Has someone been to check if Trudy's okay?"

"Someone did the first few times she went AWOL, but—"

"She does this often?" Callie was astounded.

"You could say that. Look, if I'm not needed here, can I go? I have a ton of my own work to get through today."

Callie hesitated.

"Can I ask a couple more questions before you go? I promise not to take up much time."

The nurse sighed.

"Oh well, I suppose so. Fire away."

"Was Mr Bartosz receiving intravenous treatment of any sort?"

"Like what?"

"Vitamins, chemotherapy?" Callie was struggling to think of any kind of IV therapy that might be given in a community setting. It certainly wasn't something she had ever ordered for one of her patients, unless they were in terminal care; in that case, a more permanent set-up was used.

"Nope, not that I know. He just has a dressing that needs doing a couple of times a week."

"And has he been in hospital at all recently? As an outpatient, or admitted?"

"Again, not that I know."

"Was Mr Bartosz expected to die?"

"Not really, I don't think, but, like I said, he's not my patient."

"Okay. That's fine, I can check all this with his GP, do you know who that is?"

"Dr Richardson's practice, not sure which GP though."

"Thank you." Callie's heart sank. She was going to have to face Dr Richardson and get bawled out for pinching his trainee. "You've been really helpful."

"Don't feel like I have." Anne shrugged. "He was just a rather randy old Polish guy, you know? He'd pinch your bum if you let him get near and roar with laughter if you objected, but he was okay, really."

Anne started to turn away.

"Do you know why Trudy doesn't turn up for work sometimes?" Callie asked quickly.

Anne stopped and turned back, shifting her weight from one foot to the other. It was clear she didn't really want to answer.

"It's important," Callie pushed.

"We have no proof, but the rest of us are pretty convinced that she drinks, you know? Sometimes, she slurs her words a bit, and then she just disappears, doesn't answer her phone or pick up messages, just leaves us all in the lurch. She even failed to turn up for a clinic once, but insisted she had been there, just none of the patients turned up!"

"But you haven't smelled alcohol on her breath?"

"No. Industrial strength mouthwash, yes, and she always chews extra strong mints, but, you know, if she's got a problem, I genuinely sympathise and would like to help her, but I am seriously pissed off with being landed with her work at short notice. And not just once, it's time and time again."

Callie could sympathise with that.

"Why doesn't your manager do something about it?"

"Dunno really. You'd have to ask him. He's certainly had enough complaints."

Anne hurried back to her car, leaving Callie thinking about that. She had not been impressed with how he had handled her complaint about Trudy Wells and it made sense if he had had a lot of others, both from her colleagues and from patients, but what didn't make sense was him not taking some kind of action. The nurse was clearly a liability.

* * *

Callie hadn't liked to ask Mike Parton who would be asked to do the post-mortem on Mr Bartosz, but he must have known that she would be on tenterhooks and why.

Once the coroner's officer had flagged it up as a possible crime, Callie knew that he wouldn't hand the case to Billy, as the autopsy would have to be done by a Home Office approved pathologist.

Hastings was covered by the London group practice of pathologists and of course, Professor Wadsworth was the senior member, and he had already pronounced Billy's suspicions baseless. If this case seemed to be part of a pattern, it would be impossible for him to admit he had been wrong before. And if one of the other members of the group were called upon to do the autopsy in this case, and they felt a crime had been committed, would they feel able to say so? Knowing that it would strongly suggest that the professor might just have been wrong in the previous case? At the very least they would have to ask that Billy's PM findings be checked again. And then? If they agreed with Billy, would they have the courage to overrule the great man? Cause a dispute within their consortium? Inflict damage to their own careers? Callie doubted it.

Technically, once he had looked at Parton's report, if the coroner decided that this wasn't a crime, would the case come back to Billy for him to perform the autopsy? Technically it should. And if once again, he insisted that it was murder, what would happen then?

Callie's mind was going round in circles. She had no idea what Parton and the coroner would do and it was driving her crazy. So she was very relieved to get a call from Parton, letting her know that after discussion with the coroner, and much behind-the-scenes negotiating she had no doubt, they had engaged the services of a pathologist from the West Country to do the PM. The new pathologist was already on their way from Bristol and would do it first thing in the morning.

Callie heaved a sigh of relief and thanked Parton. It really was the best possible result she could have hoped for, although she was still worried that whoever it was carrying out the post-mortem might not be keen to go up against Professor Wadsworth. He considered himself the grand old man of pathology and wasn't used to anyone questioning his judgement. She was quite sure that the coroner would have briefed the new pathologist on the dispute because it would not have been fair to let them go into this blind, even if it might have been helpful. Fingers crossed that whoever it was agreed with Billy rather than the esteemed professor!

# Chapter 18

Callie had been anxiously waiting all morning to hear from Parton or Billy about how the autopsy was going, even though she knew she was being irrational. They wouldn't have any news, not yet. Even once the autopsy had been completed, it would only be after analysis of blood samples taken during the examination that anyone would be able to say whether levels of potassium or chloride were raised. Whilst labs might be able to give a result in an hour if needed for a live patient whose life might depend on it, that rush just wouldn't happen for a dead one. But that didn't prevent her from hoping they would.

She also knew that the need to maintain the chain of evidence would slow things down even more. It might be days before the results were known and even longer before there was an official report, so there was no point worrying about it. The pathologist wouldn't want to be rushed into saying anything before he was sure. Except that Callie couldn't stop herself worrying as she sat in the doctor's office, watching the rain run down the window. She had driven to work that morning because the rain had been heavy enough to make her usual walk completely unfeasible, and it hadn't stopped all morning. It was typical British seaside summer weather.

"Hiya!" Eleanor said as she came into the room, almost dropping the pile of paperwork in her arms.

"Good morning?" Callie asked the trainee.

"Not too bad," she replied and sat at the computer station next to Callie. "How about yours?"

"Okay, I think." Callie couldn't remember much about her morning; try as she did to concentrate, she was well aware that she had drifted through the session on automatic pilot as she worried about the PM and what it might reveal. She just hoped she hadn't missed something important with any of her patients.

They both worked in silence for a while, although Callie was not getting a great deal done and was continually distracted by the rain outside and her own thoughts.

"Is everything okay?" Eleanor asked after a while. "Only, you seem a bit distracted."

"It's just all the waiting, for the results of the post-mortem." Callie shoved the remaining paperwork back into her basket. "Maybe I'll be able to concentrate better this afternoon. I need a walk to clear my head."

"What post-mortem?" Eleanor asked.

"On the old man that died yesterday. We think it might be another one."

"Another what?"

"Murder?"

"No!" Eleanor seemed shocked. "Another one all ready for a holiday? Suitcase all packed and everything?"

"Possibly," Callie admitted. "The case wasn't out ready, we found it in the cupboard, but it was packed."

"So his death might not be the same?"

"Maybe, maybe not," Callie said.

And that was the problem. She had been so sure this was another one, but what if it wasn't? She kept going over the similarities and the differences between them. The first two – or three if you counted Mrs Dingwell, which she shouldn't because she really was going away on holiday with her niece – occurred on a Tuesday. Mr Bartosz had been found on a Wednesday, although maybe that was just because he wasn't found straight away.

"We'll know more once they've finished the PM," she said, as much to herself as to Eleanor.

Eleanor looked as if she was about to say more, when Dr Grantham came in, looking grave.

"Dr Sweeting, come with me, please?" he said and left the room without so much as a nod to Callie.

Callie and Eleanor exchanged glances.

"You'd better go," Callie told the trainee and Eleanor hurried out, biting her lip as she went.

Callie gave up on her paperwork. There was too much on her mind: first waiting to hear from Mike or Billy, and now, curiosity as to what might have happened with Eleanor to make Dr Grantham so unhappy.

Callie wandered into the practice manager's office.

"What's going on?" she asked Linda.

"I'm overworked, stressed out and in need of chocolate – can you be more precise?"

Linda really did seem a bit stressed and was opening desk drawers and checking through their contents, searching for something. Callie sat down and reached for the biscuit tin. To her surprise, it was empty.

"I can tell it's been a bad day," she said. "I'll do an emergency biscuit run in a minute, but only if you tell me why Hugh has taken Eleanor into his office."

"Aha," Linda pulled a pack of indigestion tablets out of the drawer. "Too many biscuits," she explained, popping a tablet in her mouth and leaning back in her chair.

"And?" Callie persisted.

"Had a complaint about your young Dr Sweeting. First week here. It's a record."

"Oh dear." Callie's heart sank; she knew she would get the blame if Eleanor turned out to be a liability. She would have to apologise to Dr Grantham as well as Dr Richardson. "What did she do?"

"Nothing," Linda replied, "apart from telling a patient to stop wasting her time."

"Mr Herring, by any chance?"

"I wish," Linda smiled and rubbed her forehead. "I think we've all been tempted to tell Mr Herring to stop wasting our time at one point or another. No, it was that patient you've been seeing recently, Mrs Claydon."

"Monica? Why on earth did she go and see Eleanor and not me?" Callie asked. "After all, I'm the one who's referred her."

Linda shrugged, although both she and Callie knew why Monica probably had done that; she was trying every doctor in the practice in the hope that one of them would have the answer to her problems, rather than having to wait to see a hospital consultant. "And she complained?"

"Yup," Linda replied. "Can't say that I blame her – I mean, she's clearly unwell."

"Absolutely." Callie thought for a moment. "Was Eleanor just maybe trying to get her to be patient and wait for her hospital appointment?"

"You tell me." Linda shrugged as her phone began to ring and she reached for it. "Yes?" she said tersely, and Callie left her chewing another indigestion tablet and apologising to whoever was on the other end of the phone.

\* \* \*

She left the surgery with the best of intentions. The rain had stopped and she thought a walk along the shore would help clear her head, but it didn't seem to be working so she turned round and headed back to the surgery and her car. She told herself that she had a lot of visits to do anyway and she would do them quicker if she drove, but she knew that wasn't strictly true, as finding a parking space often took as long as walking to anywhere in the Old Town, where all her visits were.

Still, it was too far to walk to the hospital in her lunch break and that was where she was headed: to the mortuary. She left her car in the staff car park and hurried across the tarmac to the entrance, which was set back and a little to one side of the main hospital, next to the multi-faith chapel of rest. The mortuary door had a small and discreet sign; once inside, the corridor just led to a lift and the only choice of direction was down. Callie had been here many times before, and the place was filled with memories both good and bad, but today she was not thinking of anything from the past. She needed to know what was going on right now before she would be able to concentrate on anything else.

Down in the basement, there was an unusual amount of activity going on. She could hear voices from Billy's tiny office, but on hearing some sounds of activity coming from the sluice room, she decided to go in there first, just to check out the lie of the land. In the small room she found Jim, the mortuary technician, clearing up after the autopsy.

"Hiya," she said and was rewarded by a bright, if almost toothless, smile.

"Well, hello there, doctor, what brings you here?" Jim asked, with a twinkle in his eye that told her he knew exactly why she was there.

"Did they find anything?" she asked in a stage whisper and indicated the sealed plastic box containing a number of evidence bags, all sealed themselves, with labels signed and ready to go to the lab for forensic analysis.

"Nothing much of interest except on the back of his hand. There was what looked like tape residue there and the imprint of a peripheral IV cannula in the bruising. You know, like a Venflon or something similar, with the wings. The tissue's been sampled and swabbed."

Callie smiled with relief. That was a clear sign that someone had given him some kind of intravenous therapy, or taken blood, before he died. She knew from speaking to the nurse that he hadn't been due anything and she was sure that Dr Richardson, the nurses and the hospital records would all be checked for any legitimate reasons for the findings.

"What about time of death? Could he have died the day before he was found?"

"He hadn't fully cooled, according to the body temp taken by the forensic team, so the pathologist didn't think he could have been dead overnight."

Which meant that he must have died on the Wednesday, not Tuesday. Not quite the same as the others, then.

"And his blood is being sent off for testing too?"

"Yup." Jim nodded. "Plus samples taken from the coronary artery, cardiac muscle and intraocular fluid. All to be tested for potassium, sodium and chloride levels amongst other things."

"That's good. Very thorough."

Out in the corridor, someone called goodbye and she listened to footsteps pass the sluice door and then heard the ding of the lift arriving.

Once she was sure the coast was clear she left the sluice and headed to the office where Billy was still talking to Mike Parton.

"Hi," Billy said with a smile that showed that he too was feeling relieved that his concerns were at least being taken seriously and directly investigated.

"Did the visiting pathologist say anything?" she asked them breathlessly. "Jim told me about the signs that a cannula had been inserted into the hand. Did he talk about the blood levels of potassium?"

"He can't really, not until he has the results back, but Mike had sent him a copy of my findings from the first case, and he said that whilst the levels I found were not high enough to be definitive of a potassium chloride overdose, he felt that they were raised to a degree that meant he would have wanted further investigation."

"So, if he finds the same here?"

"It will be up to the coroner, of course, but yes, I think it might be enough for him to want to get the police involved, at least to investigate the possibility that a crime may have been committed," Parton told them.

Callie flung herself at Billy to give him a hug she was so happy. It wasn't easy in the cramped office and it meant Parton had to be uncomfortably squeezed into a corner to give her space.

"Hold on, don't go overboard. The levels may not be raised and then we are back to square one." Billy laughed.

"I don't believe that for a moment." She refused to be deflated. "We should celebrate tonight."

"We can celebrate when the results are back and the case is reopened," Billy said firmly.

"And again, when Professor Wadsworth admits he was wrong and apologises."

That made both Billy and Parton laugh; they knew there was little chance of the professor ever admitting he was wrong.

* * *

The trip to the mortuary had cheered Callie up no end, and, having grabbed a sandwich and a flat white from a café near the hospital, she breezed through her visits, dispensing prescriptions and goodwill to all. She was cutting it fine for her evening clinic by the time she got back to the surgery, but instead of going straight to her consulting room she detoured to speak to Eleanor before she started, even though it meant that both would be running late.

"Hi, Eleanor, can I have a word?" she said as she went in, and was taken aback by the angry look she got.

"If you must," Eleanor replied.

"Is something wrong?" she asked, as there quite clearly seemed to be.

"No," Eleanor replied with a look that challenged her to disagree.

Callie wasn't going to be put off that easily.

"Look, I heard about the complaint from Monica Claydon. I'm sure she didn't think she was wasting your time."

"You had already referred her; she knew there was nothing more that I could do."

"I understand that, but she probably just needed reassurance that we were doing everything we could."

"She should have trusted you. You are such a good doctor."

"Yes, of course, but when you feel that bad, sometimes you clutch at straws."

"I know. I've already had the full half-hour lecture from Dr Grantham. God, he went on and on." She rolled her eyes.

"He is an excellent doctor and a very fair man, so I hope you think hard about what he said to you," Callie said coldly.

"He treated me like a child."

She seemed genuinely angry and she left before Callie could reply that she was behaving like one.

Her attitude really irritated Callie, who was beginning to think that it might have been a mistake to offer this trainee a place here at the surgery. She was going to spend the next few weeks saying sorry to Dr Grantham, and she could only hope that she wouldn't also have to apologise to too many patients as well.

\* \* \*

When she finally got home, she was still thinking about the trainee and how she had reacted, not to the patient's complaint, but more to being spoken to by Dr Grantham about it. No one likes to be told that they have done something wrong, but Callie knew Dr Grantham well enough to know that his talk with the trainee would have been much more about discussing ways in which she could have handled the situation better, rather than direct criticism. That was how he did everything, and he always listened when you tried to explain. Considering that Eleanor had already qualified as a doctor and been through the junior doctor year in the local hospital, Callie couldn't believe that she hadn't had far worse criticism in the past. Callie could remember being publicly bawled out by a couple of surgeons, not without good cause, but that was far worse than the quiet discussion Eleanor would have had with Dr Grantham. It made her wonder if maybe Dr Richardson hadn't been as hard on Eleanor as she had made out.

As Callie dumped her bag on the sofa and headed straight for the kettle, she saw that the answer phone light was blinking.

Once she had a mug of her favourite Lady Grey tea in her hand, and had taken a healthy sip, she pressed play and listened to the message. She wasn't in the least bit surprised that it was from her mother.

"So, darling, what happened about that funny little man from the dementia charity? I'd hate to think my dramatic efforts were not being put to good use. Call me."

She really did need to follow up on that, although, now that she had told them that she no longer needed a befriender for her mother, or help caring for her, she wasn't quite sure how to approach them and find out more. Particularly now that she knew they were involved with both Mr Darling and Mrs Mount, albeit with different volunteers. The burning question was whether anyone had been visiting Mr Bartosz.

Kate had made the offer of helping with power of attorney situations and even offered her services free of charge for will writing, but so far no one had come forward with any requests.

Perhaps she could offer her own services as a befriender, or to help out in the office? She just couldn't see how on earth she could fit that in on top of everything else.

# Chapter 19

It was Sunday morning and it wasn't Callie's weekend on call for either the surgery or the police so she was surprised to be woken by her phone ringing.

Sleepily reaching for her mobile on the bedside table, she nearly knocked over the glass of water she had meant to drink before going to sleep.

"Hello?" she said groggily.

"Good morning, Callie, Steve here. Hope I didn't wake you." Miller sounded disgustingly cheery.

Callie squinted at the alarm clock on her dressing table. It said eight o'clock.

"Honestly? Yes, you did. What can I do for you?" She sat up and tried to get her brain going.

"Sorry, it's just that I thought you would want to know that we've had the preliminary results from the pathologist. On Mr Bartosz."

"Already!" Suddenly, she was wide awake.

"I know, amazing, isn't it?"

"And?" she said, frustrated that he didn't continue.

"The level of potassium and chloride in the blood, heart and particularly in the tissue surrounding the place on his hand where there was some bruising, were sky high. Even higher than Dr Iqbal's case."

"So, he's prepared to say that Mr Bartosz died as a result of an injection of potassium chloride?"

"Nothing that definite, I'm afraid, but he says he can't discount it and recommends that there should be further investigation."

"The coroner?"

"Agrees. Otherwise, it wouldn't be me calling you."

"True." If she had been more awake, and less hung-over, she would have realised that the police calling meant this was now a criminal investigation.

She let out a huge sigh of relief.

"Thank you," she said.

"You're welcome," he said. "When can you get here?"

She squinted at the clock again.

"In about half an hour," she said, "or so."

"Well, quick as you can. We need to get this investigation up and running and you seem to be the person who knows most about it."

There was a click as he put the phone down, leaving Callie muttering about days off and lie-ins to herself as she got out of bed and headed for the shower.

* * *

On her way to the police station, Callie managed to call both Billy and Parton. They had already heard the news by that time, and Callie was sure that Parton had known even earlier than her but had been waiting for a reasonable hour before calling them both.

"At least someone knows how to be considerate," she said to herself as she parked her car in one of the visitor spaces outside the police HQ and grabbed the travel mug filled with decent coffee which she had made sure to bring with her. She knew that there was unlikely to be anything remotely drinkable on offer in the station.

Callie tried not to look pleased with herself as she hurried up the stairs to the incident room, and tried to remember Billy's words of caution: "Grounds for further investigation is a long way from saying that I was right, let alone that Professor Wadsworth was wrong," but she felt she had every right to feel vindicated and couldn't help but smile as she entered the room and saw the hustle and bustle of people moving desks and setting up extra computer stations. It showed that they were increasing the size of the investigating team, anticipating that this would be a difficult case, and she was pleased that they were taking it seriously. Not that she had ever thought that they wouldn't. She knew Steve Miller well, and once he had the go-ahead to investigate, and he felt reasonably sure there had been a crime, he was always going to throw everything he could into it. He wasn't a half-hearted sort of man.

She got a wave of hello from Jayne Hales as she headed across the room towards Miller's office. On her way past, she glanced at the information boards already erected at the end of the room in readiness for the briefing Miller would be giving as soon as everyone was there. A member of the civilian staff was pinning up some pictures of Marek Bartosz's house. At the moment, his was the only name on the board but she was sure Mrs Mount was going to be added and, if she had any say in it, even Mr Darling.

Callie briefly knocked at the open door of Miller's office to get his attention. Both Miller and Jeffries were in there: Miller at his desk, looking smart and ready for work, Jeffries looking scruffy and leaning against a filing cabinet, clutching the inevitable mug of tea.

"Thanks for coming in," Miller said, standing up as she entered. "Can I get you a coffee?"

Callie waved her travel mug at him.

"All sorted, thank you." She sat in the chair opposite him. "How can I help?"

Miller hesitated.

"Let's start with Mr Bartosz, shall we? Then we can look at your concerns about the others. See if we can link all four."

"Absolutely, although I think it's only three now."

"Really? Why's that?"

"Well, one of them, June Dingwell, really was going on holiday with her niece."

"Okay." He made a note on the ad in front of him. "Anyway, let's start with Mr Bartosz. The pathologist has confirmed that there were high levels of potassium and sodium in the blood just as Dr Iqbal found with Mrs Mount. He also found a very heavy concentration in the tissue surrounding the injection site."

"That makes sense, particularly if he struggled when the injection was given."

"Yes. The pathologist said the needle or whatever, had gone through the vein and into the tissue."

"Which it might do, if he pulled his hand a way, or moved it."

"Would it hurt?" Jeffries asked. "This potassium whatsit, would it hurt when it goes in?"

"I believe so, that's one of the reasons they give it only after sedating a—" she struggled to find the right word "—um, patient when it's used in executions."

Both Miller and Jeffries gave that some thought and from the looks on their faces, it wasn't a pleasant thought.

"Do vets use it?" Miller asked. "To put down animals?"

"I don't think so, but I can check."

"What about doctors?"

"Not in high concentration and not at all in the community. We really don't give intravenous drugs in the community, unless the patient has a permanent port put in and it is part of a regimen for pain relief in terminal care or something. I have never heard of a GP giving IV potassium chloride before."

"But it is used in hospital?"

135

"It is used to treat low potassium levels, which can be bad, but because of the danger of causing the heart to stop if too strong a mix is used, or if it is given too quickly, it generally comes in ready-mixed bags of a dilute solution and is run in slowly."

"But you are saying this wasn't a dilute solution?"

"A dilute solution would take time, and it wouldn't kill, unless the patient had kidney failure or something. What was the concentration in the tissue?"

Miller passed the preliminary report to her.

"No. I don't think you could possibly get such concentrated levels around the injection site with an already diluted solution. This is way too much."

"So you don't think this is accidental?"

Callie gave it some thought.

"I honestly don't believe it can be. I cannot think of a reason why a doctor or nurse would come out into the community and give it to a patient, nor can I think of a scenario where it happened accidentally. Well, maybe once, but more than once? No."

"Is potassium chlorate a common drug to give?" Jeffries queried.

"Chloride," Callie corrected him. "Potassium chloride, and yes, it is common in IV fluids and it's sometimes added to parenteral feeds but not in these concentrations."

He gave her a look that said he didn't have a clue what she was talking about.

"If people are unable to take food orally, because they are unconscious or can't swallow, we feed them through other methods."

"A drip."

"Usually, it depends on the urgency and the reasons why someone can't eat or drink normally."

"But basically, it is available in a hospital and only there?" Miller cut in.

"Or a care home looking after long-term patients being fed like that – even in the community in some instances, but like I said, only rarely. Most people being fed parenterally are given ready-mixed food and they don't have high concentrations of potassium in them. I don't even think the hospital make their own parenteral food mix. I think they buy it in from a central place already mixed to administer."

"So why would anyone give it to this man, Mr Bartosz?"

"I don't know," Callie admitted. "He was able to eat and drink normally so I really cannot think of a single legitimate reason."

"We can check his medical records and see if they were giving him anything where it could have been a mistake," Jeffries cut in.

"You'll have to be quick, then," Callie told him. "And you'll probably need a forensic computer expert."

"What makes you say that?"

"Well, say a nurse, or doctor, did give the injection, in one or more of these cases, maybe by mistake, unlikely as that might seem, then they must have realised that they'd killed the patient. They didn't own up to it, or call for help, and there's no sign that they tried to resuscitate him. It's a career-ending mistake: killing your patient by negligence or mistake is not taken lightly."

"I'm pleased to hear it."

"But believe me, they would have erased everything from the system straight off, or made sure they didn't put anything incriminating on there in the first place."

"Could anyone do that? Delete or change the records to cover up what they had done?"

"Yes, anyone with access to the records; but I doubt they would be able to erase it permanently. Not from someone who knew what they were doing. That's why someone from forensics, an IT specialist, has to go in and check."

Miller nodded. She'd given him a reason to at least check the electronic records and see if they had been tampered with. Of course, they both knew that he'd have to persuade someone to give him a search warrant, and that wasn't going to be easy. No one liked to allow the invasion of privacy and confidentiality that would be created by checking through doctors' records.

"It would have to be a limited warrant. Just for the one patient's records, and only that one," he said, half to himself, half to remind Callie that adding in more patients, like Mr Darling and Mrs Mount, would be problematic, until they had proof in at least one of their cases.

"I understand."

Miller thought for a few moments.

"Okay, well I can at least get it started, even if it takes a while."

Callie knew there was going to be a problem finding someone with forensic IT knowledge. It wasn't like they grew on trees, and with all the emphasis on internet-based child abuse and porn, the waiting list for anything to be done was likely to be long.

"That brings us onto the other two people you think may have died the same way. Tell us about them."

"Well, there's Mrs Mount, the first one I attended."

"And the only other one to have a post-mortem."

"Exactly."

"Any differences between her and Mr Bartosz?"

"The site," she said.

"They were both killed in their own homes, weren't they?" Jeffries queried.

"Injection site," she clarified. "In Mrs Mount's case, the vein at the elbow was used and there was no sign of any kind of cannula, just a normal needle."

"Why would the killer change methods?"

"Maybe because it was hard to keep her still while the injection was given. There was a very big bruise at the site."

"This cannula thing, where would you get one of those?"

Callie smiled.

"Well, it's not something most people would have, but it's commonly used in hospitals, and out in the community. It can be hard getting blood samples from old people; their veins aren't in good condition and tend to collapse, so sometimes it's easier, if you have many samples or are giving doses of something intravenously, to use one of these cannulas, and to choose the veins on the back of the hand or the wrist, as with Mr Bartosz."

"You think it's someone with medical knowledge?"

"I do think that's likely, yes."

"And you think the killer is learning as they go along?" Jeffries asked her.

"Finding easier ways of doing the injection, and trying to cover up what's happened by hiding the suitcase like with Mr Bartosz? Yes. Yes I do."

They all sat in silence. It was a horrifying thought, because, if the killer was getting better at covering their tracks, then how would they know if there was another victim?

# Chapter 20

The unexpected trip to the police station meant that Callie was running late for her regular brunch date with Kate. She rang Billy as she hurried from the parking spot she had eventually found, a considerable distance from her destination in the Old Town, and told him about her meeting with Miller as she walked to the café.

"I can't remember ever seeing potassium chloride used except in a very much diluted solution. How would you go about getting hold of a strong one in hospital?" she asked him.

"With difficulty, is the short answer. It's held in the pharmacy and they treat it like a controlled drug. You have to sign for it and it's on a named-patient basis only. You can't just sign out a load in case you might need it."

"I didn't think it would be easy."

"I did a bit of research and most pharmaceutical companies will only supply it to medical institutions or places licensed for making up parenteral feeds as well. You can't just go into a chemist and ask for it."

"You could make up your own, I suppose."

"Yes, you can get tablets or powder quite easily and, of course, you can get it online. It's dirt cheap on eBay."

"On eBay?"

"They sell it as a food supplement."

Callie sighed; it was depressing to know how easy it was to get hold of it. The good news was that Parton had arranged for Mrs Mount to have a second post-mortem, done by the same man who had come to perform the one on Mr Bartosz.

"I've asked him to check for any signs that her arm was restrained as well, any bruising might not have been visible straight after death but might be more easily identified now," he had added.

Callie cheered up; things were definitely moving in the right direction.

Having arrived at the café she hurried inside, just in time to see a large plate of fried food being put down in front of Kate.

"You're late," her friend said, squeezing a generous dollop of tomato ketchup onto the side of the plate.

"Sorry." Callie sat down. Kate put a large forkful of bacon into her mouth and moaned in pleasure, making Callie and the waitress smile.

"The usual?" the waitress asked Callie. "Or what you had the other day?"

"Usual please. No hangover today," she answered with a smile.

"What's your excuse then?" Kate asked her friend, once she had finished her mouthful.

"I was at the police station, briefing Steve on potassium chloride poisoning."

Kate stopped eating and waved a forkful of sausage at Callie.

"Does that mean they are taking this seriously now?"

"It does."

"Well done! You managed to get them to change their minds?"

"Not me, no." Callie shook her head. "The independent pathologist did. He wasn't happy to classify the latest one as natural causes."

"Unlike the dear professor."

"Indeed, and he's doing another PM on the first lady too."

They stopped talking as the waitress brought a pot of Lady Grey tea for Callie.

"Cheers." Kate raised her mug. Callie quickly poured out some tea and raised hers in reply.

"Cheers."

"Did you tell them about your little escapade with the charity?"

"No."

"Why not?"

"Because it's becoming more apparent that the person doing this has medical knowledge." She told her friend about the cannula in the back of Mr Bartosz's hand.

"You're back to thinking about the nurse?"

"It seems the most likely explanation. I mean, we know she was visiting, or supposed to be visiting, at least two of the victims. She has to be worth talking to, at the very least. Steve promised me they would look into her, and the rest of the community nursing team."

"Speaking of the charity, they have asked me to sort out a power of attorney for one of their clients. It all seems quite kosher and it's not for them to have the power but for a family member, so I've set up an appointment to get the ball rolling."

"I'm sorry to have dragged you into more work, particularly as it doesn't seem to be connected to the deaths anymore."

"Don't worry about it. I'm glad to help out if they are genuine and if I have any concerns, I'll let you know." She wiped some toast around her plate to get the last of the egg yolk. "As well as the appropriate authorities, of course."

They both paused as the waitress set down a plate of buttery scrambled eggs and smoked salmon in front of Callie, and a fresh rack of wholemeal toast. Kate took a slice of the fresh toast and slathered it with butter and marmalade.

"I love this place," Callie said as she suddenly realised just how hungry she was. For a few minutes neither said anything as they tucked into their food.

"Steve's also started the process of getting a warrant for the medical records," she said once both she and Kate had finished eating.

"Can't see that happening any time soon," Kate commented. "They might be able to get hold of the latest victim's, but no one is going to allow them access to multiple patient records, let alone do a more generalised trawl."

Callie knew that she was probably right.

"At least if they find anything untoward with the first set of records, it might be enough to get a slightly wider warrant granted."

Kate nodded her agreement and poured the last of the coffee from the cafetière into her mug. Callie similarly topped up her tea.

"So, if the pathologist is redoing the first post-mortem, and the police are investigating both the latest deaths where there might, or might not, be some evidence for them to find, there's nothing more for you to do now, is there?"

Kate's eyes were twinkling as she said this, because she knew that Callie could never resist the opportunity to do a bit of sleuthing on her own.

"Well…" Callie's hesitation confirmed her friend's suspicions. "I had thought I might have a word with a few of the other nurses working in the community, see if I could find out more about my particular bête noire and why she still has a job."

"It's very hard to sack someone in the NHS."

"I know, but going AWOL and drinking on duty are probably grounds enough – at least, I would hope so."

"That's if she really has done those things," Kate cautioned. "You only have one other nurse's word for that."

"True," Callie conceded. "I suppose you never know. I might find out that despite my own experience, she's a dedicated professional and the other nurse was lying about her out of jealousy."

Callie very much doubted it, but it was something she had to check out in fairness to Trudy Wells.

"But if it's all true, then she has to have some sort of a hold over her manager, something that means he can't get rid of her," Kate said.

"Exactly."

"Like what, though?"

"I'm betting it's something to do with money, embezzling, false claims, misappropriation of funds..."

"Yes, that makes sense." Kate nodded in agreement, then grinned. "Or perhaps it's a sexual hold. He's obsessed by her body? Or maybe he's been sleeping with a patient and she's blackmailing him?"

Callie looked appalled.

"I really can't even begin to believe those two scenarios. I'm going to concentrate on the financial angle, and I think I know who might be able to get that information for me." Callie smiled.

"Who?"

But Callie said nothing; just tapped the side of her nose.

* * *

Callie had intimated to Kate that she had a source for information about the financial side of Hastings Care, the social enterprise that ran both the community nursing teams and also the carers. In reality, she had little more than an acquaintance with someone and no idea if they would actually be able or want to help her.

Amanda Ayling was a one-time health visitor who had worked with Callie in the past, in particular with a family who had been unable to care adequately for their children. She had struck Callie then as someone who sincerely cared for her clients and who strove to do her best for them. A slim, middle-aged lady, frighteningly efficient and a renowned hard worker, she always put a hundred per cent into everything she took on. She had moved away from seeing clients herself soon after the case that had brought them together, and had managed the health visiting team for some years before making another change of direction when she joined Hastings Care, where she was in charge of compliance and was also a board member.

Callie had decided that meeting in the care team offices was probably not the best idea, considering what she was going to ask, so when she rang Amanda first thing Monday morning, she suggested going for coffee and a sandwich in a nearby café for lunch. She was surprised when Amanda agreed.

Certain that Amanda would be punctual, just because that's the sort of person she was, Callie made sure she was there in good time and found a seat in a quiet corner where she could watch the door, and ordered a coffee for herself.

True to form, Amanda arrived, exactly on time, and Callie waved her over. She didn't look a day older than the last time they had met, despite her hair now being a steely grey. It was cut in a neat practical style and the grey suited her. She was wearing a dark blue A-line skirt, with a matching scarf over her white blouse, and had a large laptop case with her, no doubt also full of notebooks, pens that worked and other useful items. She managed to make Callie feel slightly inadequate.

"Callie, lovely to see you," Amanda said, sitting down opposite Callie and carefully placing the laptop bag next to her chair and out of the way of other customers. "How can I help you?"

Callie hesitated. She had given a considerable amount of thought to how she could approach this conversation and had come to the conclusion that honesty was the best policy. However, that didn't make her any more confident of persuading Amanda to do what she was asking. Callie fully expected her to refuse to help; after all, it probably wasn't in her best interest to do so, and it certainly wasn't in the interests of Hastings Care. So she carefully explained about the deaths, and how she, and now the police, were concerned that there might be a link.

Amanda frowned as they paused to order coffee and sandwiches. As soon as the waitress had moved away, Callie braced herself for bad news.

"The police contacted us this morning," Amanda admitted, "although they only told us they were investigating the circumstances around the death of one patient."

Callie coloured slightly. Perhaps she should not have suggested that there were more than that.

"But," Amanda continued, "from what you have said, it might just be a matter of time before they broaden their investigation."

"Yes, I believe so," Callie agreed. "And there is something else you should know."

Amanda raised a questioning eyebrow, encouraging Callie to tell her more, and once the coffee had been delivered and the waitress was safely out of earshot, Callie told her about her concerns regarding the nurse, Trudy Wells, who had visited at least two of the victims. She also mentioned, without dropping the other nurse in it, the rumours she had heard about Trudy disappearing for periods and possibly drinking on duty.

"What I don't understand," Callie said, "is why she is still employed at Hastings Care, given the complaints about the standard of her work, and from her colleagues."

There was a pause, punctuated only by a long sigh from Amanda as she thought about the news she had just heard.

"Dr Hughes, Callie, this is perhaps more what I was expecting from you – until the police were in touch this morning, that is – but I had no idea that it was anywhere as bad as this."

"But you knew something was wrong?"

"Yes, yes, it had become clear that there were problems, and I had raised a number of concerns at the last board meeting."

"There have been other complaints?"

"I really can't tell you, it's unfair, not just on the nurse concerned and also on her manager, but on Hastings Care, too." She shook her head as she thought about it, and then made a decision. "You have my word that I will investigate this and I will of course speak to the nursing team to see if I can find out what is going on there, before confronting her manager if needs be. I will also ensure that we co-operate fully with the police, I know you would expect nothing less, if only to prove that we have nothing to do with the deaths." She paused and looked Callie in the eye. "My question to you is, what else do you need from us?"

This was more than Callie had been expecting and the offer of further help took her by surprise. She thought for a moment before answering.

"If there is a connection between these deaths, I'd like to know if there have been others your nursing team have concerns about, and if so, why? And in each case, which nurse was visiting."

"Yes," Amanda nodded. "I can get that information for you. The fact that you are a doctor will help override concerns about confidentiality, although" – she hesitated – "you must understand that I have an obligation to both Hastings Care, and, more importantly, the staff. If Nurse Wells has a problem, I need to get help for her and if her manager has not been doing his job, I need to find out why and deal with it internally and you will just have to accept that."

Callie nodded her agreement.

"But if you find out there is a connection to the deaths?"

"I will tell the police, of course. Apart from anything else, Hastings Care would not survive under those circumstances. Our contracts would be terminated, I have no doubt. In which case, my priority would be ensuring continuity of care for our clients whilst a new social enterprise was set up, or an outside company took over."

Her face told Callie that one of the bigger companies providing care services might have already made an offer to take over the service, and that a takeover wasn't what Amanda, or, for that matter, Callie, would want.

# Chapter 21

Halfway through her busy Monday morning surgery, Callie's mobile buzzed, letting her know that she had an incoming call. She glanced briefly at it and noted that it was from Billy, but didn't answer as she had a patient with her. As soon as the patient left, she listened to the voicemail he had left which just said, "Call me as soon as possible." Callie thought he sounded excited. She tried but got his voicemail, and left a similar message for him. She didn't have to wait too long to find out what had caused his excitement because her telephone rang again before she could call her next patient through, but it wasn't Billy, it was Mike Parton.

"Just had word about the review of Mrs Mount's PM and Dr Iqbal's findings," he told her.

"And the external pathologist agrees with Billy? That it was murder?"

"I wouldn't go as far as to say that." Parton was maddeningly precise. "He just says again that he thinks there are grounds for further investigation as he cannot rule it out."

The pathologist might not have been specific about murder, but he had gone against Professor Wadsworth and that was brave. Callie was so delighted that if he had been in the room she would have jumped up and given him a hug, so perhaps it was just as well he wasn't there, or Parton for that matter, as she would probably have hugged him too.

At the end of surgery, she would make a quick dash over to the mortuary so she could give Billy a hug instead.

\* \* \*

On Monday afternoon, having managed to fit in a trip to the mortuary as well as her home visits, Callie took the time to speak to Dr Grantham in his consulting room before he started his evening surgery.

"Do you have a minute, Hugh?" she asked.

"For you, Callie? Always," he said with a not entirely sincere smile, waving her to come in and sit down.

"I just wanted to apologise."

"What on earth for?" He seemed genuinely puzzled.

"I persuaded you to take on Eleanor, because of the problems she was having at her previous surgery and now I understand that there's been a complaint."

Dr Grantham sighed.

"It's hardly your fault, Callie. After all, I was the one who spoke to Dr Richardson and he did try to warn me off, said that he had concerns about her, but I thought it was just further evidence that her placement was breaking down."

"And now?"

"Who knows?" He shrugged. "It's down to her, but from the way she responded to my very gentle criticism and suggestions on ways she could have handled things better, I have to admit that I am concerned."

"You would have thought she would have learned to take criticism by now."

"Indeed. Do you have any suggestions?"

"I am sure you are the best person to get through to her." Callie really didn't want to get involved with the training, if she could possibly help it, even if she was partly to blame. "I thought I would pop in and see Monica Claydon, see if I can smooth things over there, reassure her that we are doing everything that we can."

Dr Grantham nodded.

"That would be a good start, but I was thinking more about supervising young Eleanor." He looked at Callie; he wasn't going to let her off the hook. "I think we probably need to go back a bit, to doing consultations with one of us there."

"That really is almost back to the beginning!"

Callie was surprised. New trainees started by simply sitting in on surgeries done by their trainer, then did their own consultations in a trainer's presence, and finally moved on to seeing patients alone, but having a certain number of consultations videoed for review with the supervisor. In the final few months of training, the new doctor was able to see patients entirely alone, but would discuss afterwards what actions had or had not been taken, and that was where Eleanor was, or should have been. Callie knew it was always hard finding patients who were happy to have their consultations recorded, no matter how much reassurance they were given that it was purely for training purposes and would only be reviewed by Dr Grantham and the trainee. The patients seemed to imagine that the staff sat round giggling at their problems or, heaven forbid, their overweight, hairy and/or pallid bodies.

"Hmm, she wasn't keen." His tone indicated that this had been a difficult discussion. "In the end we compromised on her recording as many patients as she could persuade to let her for this week so that we could go over them."

"That seems reasonable."

"She didn't seem to think so," he said drily.

"Ah, well, I suppose it seems like a step back."

"That's because it is."

"She must feel like she's being punished."

Dr Grantham sighed.

"I do understand, Callie, but, as I did try and explain to Eleanor, it isn't a punishment, even though the way she spoke to her patient was not acceptable. It's to help her learn better ways of talking to people, getting them to do what you want them to do, without being angry or rude."

Callie knew he was right, that it would have been better, and more successful, if Eleanor had simply reassured Monica Claydon that everything that could be done was being done, as quickly as it could, and that there was no point in her coming in and pestering the doctors. But equally, Callie didn't know any doctors who didn't occasionally lose it to the degree that they told a patient a few home truths, at least at some point in their career. Except possibly for Dr Grantham; she had never seen him anything but polite, concerned and caring. Which was probably why his patients loved him so much.

\* \* \*

Monica Claydon's house was just how Callie had imagined it would be. Modern and practical, with a small front garden and a parking space for a small and practical hatchback. At first glance, everything looked neat and cared for, but on closer inspection Callie could see that one or two things had been allowed to slip. The car could do with a clean, some plants had died, weeds were beginning to take over, and, when she reached the front door, she could see that the windows needed cleaning and the milk was still on the step.

Callie rang the bell and waited until she heard Monica call out, "Coming!"

The door finally opened and Monica stood there, one hand covering the left side of her face and holding a tissue.

"Dr Hughes?" She seemed confused to see her.

"Hello, Monica, I know it's late but I thought I would come round and see how you are. Can I come in?"

Monica stood back to let her in, hand still up at her face. Callie waited patiently as she closed the door and led the way into the sitting room. The room was neat and tidy, apart from around one chair, clearly where Monica usually sat. The armchair was positioned so that she could watch the television and had a small table next to it. The table was covered with newspapers, plates and used cups, while the rubbish bin next to it was full of biscuit wrappers and other rubbish. It all told Callie that her patient was not eating properly. Too ill to cook, she was surviving on a diet of easy food: sandwiches, microwave meals and junk.

Callie sat on the sofa, and Monica sank into her chair, hand still on her face.

"I'm sorry about the mess," she said, with difficulty.

"No, I'm sorry. This" – she pointed at the overflowing bin – "tells me you are struggling and I understand, I really do."

Monica nodded.

"Is there something wrong with your face, Monica?" she asked. "Can you take your hand away?"

Monica did as asked and dropped her hand.

Callie could see that the left-hand side of Monica's face had drooped from the lower eyelid, all the way down to her mouth which was dribbling slightly, which was presumably why she was clutching a tissue to it. Callie crossed the room and bent down to get a closer look and touched her left cheek.

"Does it feel odd?" Callie asked. "Numb or tingly?"

Monica shook her head.

"Not really, not numb when I touch it, but it feels wrong somehow."

Callie continued her examination of the patient by checking that her pupils were reacting.

"Headache?"

"No more than usual."

Speaking was obviously hard and Callie could see that the left side of her patient's mouth was not moving at all.

She went through the process of checking Monica for signs of other weakness on the left side of her body or anything that might indicate a stroke, but the problem seemed limited to the left side of her face.

"And can you raise your eyebrows?"

Monica tried, but only her right eyebrow lifted.

"And show me your teeth."

Only the right side of Monica's mouth responded to her trying to do this.

"Can you close your eyes?"

Again, only her right eye closed properly.

Callie went back to her seat and Monica brought her hand up, dabbing at her mouth with a tissue.

"When did you notice this?"

"When I woke up."

"This morning?"

"No, about an hour ago. I fell asleep in my chair." Monica burst into tears. "I'm sorry, but I was so worried, I didn't know what to do."

Callie hurried back across the room to comfort her.

"Have I had a stroke, doctor?" Monica asked once she had stopped sobbing.

"No, no, I don't think so. It's much more likely to be something called Bell's palsy," Callie reassured the tearful woman.

"But why has it happened now, when I'm already feeling so awful?"

"Well. Things often happen together. When your immunity is low, other illnesses strike. That's only natural." But in the back of Callie's mind, there was something telling her of a link between particular illnesses and Bell's palsy.

Once Monica had calmed down, Callie went to her bag and brought out a packet of tablets.

"I'm going to leave you with three days' supply of steroids, which should help reduce the inflammation that's causing this. I'll also give you a prescription for some more steroids and some eye drops as your eye will get very dry with you not being able to close it or blink."

"It feels sore."

"You may find that taping it shut when you sleep will help protect it. Do you have any micropore tape or something like it?"

"Yes, I think so, in the first aid kit I keep."

"Well, that's best as it's gentle on the skin."

Callie put the packet of tablets and a prescription on the table next to Monica's chair.

"I want you to take six tablets now, with something to eat, and the same in the morning with breakfast and then come and see me. I'll fit you in, whatever time you can get to surgery in the morning." Callie stood.

"Do you know what's causing it then, doctor?"

"I'm not sure," Callie told her, honestly. "And I need to check a few things, I read a report about possibly using antiviral medication as well as steroids, so I'll look it up and I can prescribe them tomorrow if there's any evidence that they help." Callie stood up to leave.

"Thank you, thank you so much." Monica struggled to get up.

"No, no, stay where you are, I can see myself out," Callie said hastily. "And I'm going to speak to the consultant I referred you to. It's probably too late tonight, but I'll try first thing in the morning. He may suggest more tests, or even a change of treatment, but either way, I want to see you tomorrow, okay?"

Monica nodded.

"If you're not well enough to come in, I'll come back here, just let me know."

Once she had left, Callie hurried home. There were things she had to check, and despite what she had said to Monica, she might try and call the consultant that night; after all, there was a possibility he could be on duty, but she didn't hold out much hope. She also wanted to check about antivirals, and there was still something niggling that she might have read about a connection between systemic symptoms and Bell's palsy. It would be fantastic if she could find something that fitted with all of Monica's symptoms, particularly if it was something she could treat.

# Chapter 22

If the receptionist was surprised to see Callie at the surgery so early, she hid it well and just called out a cheery "Good morning!" as she continued setting up for the busy day ahead.

Callie responded quickly and continued on her way up to the office. As expected, she had not been able to get hold of the hospital consultant the night before, but some online research had given her the information she had been trying so desperately to remember when she saw Monica: insect bites, particularly from fleas, could cause Lyme disease. Usually, a few days or weeks after the bite, a diagnostic "bull's-eye" rash could be seen before symptoms appeared, but with Monica's dark skin tone, she might have missed the signs. Once the rash had disappeared, the bacterial infection could cause generalised illness, particularly tiredness, joint pains, and, what had jogged her memory the night before, a palsy of the facial muscles.

As soon as Callie was at a desk in the main office, she picked up the phone and called Monica. She had thought about calling earlier, or even popping in on her way to work, but decided it was unfair on the poor woman who was already exhausted, to wake her up. However, she really needed to talk to her patient before trying the consultant again. Callie needed confirmation that her theory was, at least, possible, because, if she was right, Monica needed to start antibiotics as soon as possible.

"Hello?" Callie asked as a rather groggy Monica answered her phone, eventually.

"Hi, Monica, it's Dr Hughes, I just wanted to ask you a couple of questions before I try and get hold of anyone at the hospital, if that's all right?"

"Yes, of course. What do you need to know?" Her voice still sounded a little slurred, so she was probably still having problems from the Bell's palsy, Callie thought.

"Can you tell me, did you go for country walks before you got ill?"

"Well, yes, doctor. I used to call it hiking, but it was just long walks usually. Helped to keep me fit."

"Absolutely. So when was the last time you went for a hike? And where was it?"

If Monica was surprised by the line of questioning, she hid it well.

"Well, they were more like long walks than hikes really I suppose. Every weekend, if the weather was fair, I'd pack a rucksack, and spend the day walking the South Downs. I love it up there, but it's been a few months since I last felt able to do it." Monica thought for a moment. "Last time must have been about three months ago now."

"And you don't remember getting bitten at all or finding any insects on you?"

"No. Nothing at all." Monica paused. "Can you tell me why you are asking doctor?"

Callie explained that ticks could spread a bacterial infection called Lyme disease and about how her research on it the night before had matched Monica's symptoms.

"And it's treatable?" Monica asked, in a hopeful voice.

"Yes, if that is what you have, then it is, but I need to sort out a blood test for you and also speak to the consultant, so I'll get onto the hospital now and then let you know what he says."

Callie finished the call and immediately rang the hospital, hoping she would catch the doctor before he started morning rounds. She refused to be distracted by Linda, who had placed a bunch of paperwork in front of her.

"How come you're in so early?" Linda asked as Callie waited to be put through.

"Because I had a lot to do," Callie answered.

"Not to do your paperwork then?" Linda looked pointedly at the pile she had just placed on the desk. Callie didn't manage to answer, because, much to her surprise, she managed to get hold of the consultant straight away, and quickly told him about Monica and the development of Bell's palsy and her thoughts on what might have caused it.

"That sounds reasonable," he said once she had finished and she had to hide her disappointment. She felt that her deduction warranted a much bigger response than just reasonable. Brilliant and inspired, came to mind.

She sighed as she put down the phone. Still, at least he had agreed to check Monica for it and said he would email over the blood test request form later that morning. Once the blood had been taken, she should start on a course of antibiotics, he had told Callie, and also advised her on the choice and length of treatment. He had suggested not starting them until they had confirmation that she had the disease, but Callie was so sure of her diagnosis she had decided to start the antibiotics as soon as the blood had been taken to test for it. She knew that some doctors would say she shouldn't, because there were always risks in doing so, not to mention costs, but she felt that Monica had been ill long enough, and the longer she went without treatment, the more it became likely that she might have long-term effects from the disease.

"Well done, Dr Hughes, that definitely deserves a pat on the back," Linda said once Callie had finished the call.

"And a cup of coffee?" Callie asked.

"Only if you sign all of those." Linda indicated the pile she had placed on the desk. "And you never know, I might even let you have a chocolate biscuit to go with it."

* * *

Morning surgery had almost finished when Monica came in to see Callie, who gave her the form she needed to have the special test that would confirm, or disprove, Lyme disease.

"The test needs to be taken at the hospital; the phlebotomy department is in outpatients."

"I know where that is," Monica told her. "Been there a few times." She smiled. "Thank you so much, doctor, I can't tell you how much better I feel just knowing what it is I have."

"Well, we don't know for sure, not until we get the test result, and even then, it might not be conclusive."

Callie was worried her patient would set too much store by her tentative diagnosis, no matter how convinced she herself was. She knew that if she was wrong, it would be a huge blow for Monica.

"Don't start them until after you've had the test." Callie told her as she also handed over a prescription for some antibiotics. "Just in case it muddies the water."

Once her last patient of the morning had gone, Callie gave some thought to Eleanor. Would the trainee take it as further criticism if Callie told her about the possible diagnosis she had made? It was an interesting case and it might even make a good one to present at one of the medical meetings. Callie thought perhaps she should ask Dr Grantham what he thought, after all, he was still the official trainer.

When Callie went into the office, Dr Grantham was sitting on one side of the room and Eleanor was on the other, packing up her things and logging out of her computer.

"Finished already?" Callie said brightly. Eleanor seemed about to say something in reply but then glanced at Dr Grantham and decided not to say anything. She picked up her things and left.

Callie could have followed but decided against it, if Eleanor didn't want to talk in front of her trainer, then Callie didn't think she should interfere.

"Oh dear," Callie said.

"She's sulking," Dr Grantham explained, unnecessarily. "Just like my youngest used to. Only she'd grown out of it by the time she was eighteen."

He studiously returned to his paperwork, cutting off any further discussion.

Callie was sad that her earlier belief that Eleanor would make a good GP was proving wrong. She wouldn't survive in the job for long if she took advice so personally, and there was no way Dr Grantham was going to recruit her to their practice once she qualified now he had seen this side of her. And the fact that she had moved practices and that neither was willing to offer her a job would count against her when she applied elsewhere, Callie was sure. Particularly as it was well known that they were one partner short and having little success recruiting someone permanent to help.

She was saved from having to make any further comment about the situation as her mobile phone rang. She hurried out of the room to answer it, not wanting to disturb the senior partner any more than he had been already.

A quick glance at caller ID told her that it was Steve Miller calling and she knew Dr Grantham would be further irritated that her other job was intruding on her work as a GP. He really wanted her to take the vacant partner post and commit to working at the practice full time.

"Hello, Steve," she said.

"Hi, Callie, I was wondering if I could call upon your expertise."

"Of course. How can I help?"

"I put in for a warrant to get the medical records for Marek Bartosz as you suggested—"

"Are you going to add Elizabeth Mount to the request now that the new pathologist has suggested her death needs further investigation?" she interrupted.

"Already have," he replied, "and the warrant has been granted, so I'll be asking the relevant surgeries to send them over this afternoon."

"Fantastic!"

"Well, yes, but I'm not sure how much they'll tell us," he told her.

"I suspect it's more about what they don't tell us."

"How do you mean?"

"Like if no one has requested a visit or a blood test on the relevant day. Or that there was no record of any reason why they would need a test or any kind of intravenous therapy. So, if there's no legitimate reason for them to have those tests or treatments, why did they have the marks?"

"And who better to tell me what is or isn't in the records, than a doctor."

"Ah, I see." She understood the reason for his call. "I take it you would you like me to take a look at them once they arrive?"

"That would be very helpful," he agreed, sounding relieved to have persuaded her so easily. Callie wasn't about to tell him that wild horses wouldn't have kept her away from examining those notes.

* * *

The medical records of Marek Bartosz and Elizabeth Mount were emailed over to the police station during the afternoon and Miller sent Callie a text saying he would print them out and come to her flat later that evening to give them to her. She composed a reply, saying he could drop them at the surgery, but as she wrote it, she realised that he might not be finished in time. He could send someone else with the confidential medical records, of course, but might not want to in case they went astray. Or maybe he just wanted to see her? Whatever his reason for bringing them in person, she decided that she would be quite happy to see him. With that in mind, she erased her original text and just sent him an acknowledgement, resisting the urge to put a smiley face or a cross at the bottom. After all, she was still going out with Billy, who might or might not be leaving Hastings, and her, while Miller was still, technically, married. It really wouldn't do to give him any encouragement.

# Chapter 23

On her way home from the surgery, Callie stopped at a convenience store to stock up on fresh milk and a few other essentials, such as a bottle of wine, some plain chocolate digestives and a bumper pack of crisps. On the hospitality front, she felt confident she had covered all the bases Miller would expect. He knew she wasn't particularly domesticated, even if her cupboards were certainly better filled these days, if only because Billy brought supplies with him. If Miller wanted anything more substantial to eat, and experience had taught her that he wouldn't have found time to do so while at work, they'd have to order a takeaway. Or go out.

Once home, she put away her shopping, pouring herself a glass of wine before placing the bottle in the fridge, and took her laptop over to the sofa. She clicked on the television, and half listened to a news channel as she caught up on personal emails.

Miller still hadn't arrived when she had finished both her emails and the wine, so she refilled her glass, opened the crisps and decided to go over the notes she had on the two deaths that were currently under investigation. Her conviction that the deaths were occurring at two weekly intervals had been undermined by the change of day on which Bartosz had been killed, and the fact that there were now only two who had died on a Tuesday and one on a Wednesday. Callie wondered about that; perhaps the killer was trying to throw them off the scent by changing the day. Perhaps they had hidden the suitcase in the cupboard at the Bartosz scene for the same reason, so it wouldn't be seen straight away and maybe not until the house was cleared much later.

The more she thought about it, the more she realised that the killer was possibly adapting in order to stop the police from noticing that there was a pattern and that these deaths were connected. What had made them change? At the time Mr Bartosz died, the police weren't connecting the deaths; indeed, the official line was that they were due to natural causes. She, Callie, was the only person who had connected them. Could the killer have heard about her interest? And if so, how?

Callie jumped as her thoughts were interrupted by the doorbell and she got up to let Miller in.

She barely registered how drawn and tired he looked as he thrust a bottle of her favourite wine at her, along with a bag that was giving off the delicious aromas of Indian cuisine.

"The killer knows we're onto them," she said as she hurried to her open-plan kitchen area. She put the wine in the fridge, getting out the opened bottle and handing Miller a glass.

"What do you mean?" he asked as he poured himself some wine, but she had been temporarily distracted by the food she was unpacking.

"Oh wow, onion bhajis. And poppadoms!"

She looked up, suddenly realising that he had spoken.

"What did you say?"

"I asked, what do you mean? About the killer knowing that we are onto them?" Miller repeated as he watched her open the containers, smiling at her enthusiasm. "You must be hungry."

"Very," she agreed, handing him a plate as she began ladling butter chicken onto her own. "You'd better grab some of this before I eat the lot."

She waited until he had filled his plate as well, before answering his question.

"The killer has changed what they are doing," she explained, telling him about the way the suitcase had been hidden and the day the murders occurred had changed.

"Or it might just have occurred to him that we would piece it all together if he didn't change it."

"Or her," she corrected him.

"Of course. He, she or they may have guessed that we would piece it together."

"True, they may have," she conceded. "But what if they heard that the police were already interested in the murders of older people who were about to go on holiday?"

"How would they know that? We weren't."

"But they might know I was interested in them, because I asked about it at the LMC meeting."

Miller chewed thoughtfully for a moment.

"Who exactly goes to those meetings?" Miller asked her.

"Local GPs," she said, "and an occasional practice manager or spouse, but generally it's just the GPs."

"So, it would only be a doctor who knew about your interest then?"

"Or anyone they told. They might have asked their practice manager to ask around about it, or run a check on old people who'd died unexpectedly or something."

Miller thought about it some more and Callie took the opportunity to claim the last poppadom.

"This is delicious." She scraped the raita and chutney dishes onto her plate as well. Miller knew better than to complain; besides, he'd had the lion's share of the curry and rice.

"Do you think the change of day is part of that attempt to stop us, or you, from connecting them?" he asked her between mouthfuls.

"I don't know," she admitted, "it could be."

"Or it might just indicate a normal change in shift pattern. Like with a nurse, so they can cover evenings and weekends."

"Yes." She thought for a while. "Although I'm fairly sure they have set workdays and times. Most of them have families and need to organise childcare and such like and some people prefer to work weekends or nights. But I can ask someone I know how it works. She'll be able to tell me who was working on the dates in question and if anyone has requested to change their days off."

Callie was sure Amanda would be able to help her with that, and it would give her an excuse to ask how the investigation into Trudy Wells was going.

"And if it's a nurse, or something similar," Miller continued, "could they do it while on duty? Then their day off would be irrelevant."

It was another good point, Callie had to concede, and not one she had given much thought to. He was right; a nurse could be carrying out the murders while actually on duty, provided they worked alone. That way, their presence wouldn't be questioned.

"Have you thought about going to the press?" she asked.

"No," he replied firmly.

"No, you haven't given it any thought, or no it's not going to happen?"

"Both."

"Well, that can't be true," Callie chided him good-naturedly.

"Okay, so I gave a passing thought to alerting people to our concerns, but as we have nothing concrete, we could just be causing unnecessary anxiety."

"But you might find more cases."

"And make even more work for ourselves."

"Or less, if one of them is easier to prove, or gives you a better idea of a pattern."

"And meanwhile, we would have caused mass panic amongst the elderly. No" – he shook his head to emphasise his point – "the Chief Super would never agree to it, so there's no point in my even raising it. The time might come in the future, but for now, until we have more of an idea of what's going on, no speaking to the press."

"Even if that means a death that might have been prevented if you had warned people?"

He sighed.

"You know as well as I do that there are no right decisions here. If we scare people now and there are no more deaths, we will be accused of overreacting, if we don't and someone dies, we won't have done enough. I can't go public until we have more evidence."

Callie knew that his tone meant there was no point going on about it. His mind was made up and she couldn't really blame him. They carried on eating in silence for a while.

"How's things at home?" she asked eventually.

"Lizzie has started divorce proceedings."

"I'm sorry to hear that."

He shrugged it off.

Callie knew that his wife had moved out following a miscarriage for which she blamed Miller and, indirectly, Callie, but she had hoped that once the dust had settled, she might have changed her mind.

"Is there any hope of her reconsidering?"

"No." He shook his head. "And I'm not really sure that I want her to."

She understood. It had always been a difficult marriage, but Miller had loved his wife, of that she was certain, and this could not have been an easy time.

"How's things with you and Billy?" he asked.

"Oh, fine," she answered. Not wishing to go into the possibility of him moving to Northern Ireland, or to discuss whether or not she'd go with him. Now really wasn't the time.

Once they had finished their food and were settled on the sofa with cups of coffee in front of them, Callie held out her hand.

"Medical records?"

He went to his coat and pulled out a bunch of printed sheets.

"Here," he said as she took them from him.

He sat and sipped his coffee, watching her as she read the printouts, frowning as she concentrated, sometimes shuffling backwards or forwards through them to check things. It was warm in the room, and he'd just eaten a large meal, not to mention drunk two glasses of wine, so perhaps it wasn't surprising that by the time Callie had finished looking through the notes, he had nodded off to sleep.

# Chapter 24

Next morning, Callie straightened the living room whilst she waited for the kettle to boil. Not that it needed much straightening. Miller had spent the night on the sofa, covered with a blanket, and Callie had woken to the sound of him pottering round, clearing up the remains of their dinner. By the time she got up, he had left and the room was as neat as always. He had even neatly folded the blanket and taken the rubbish out when he went. She had only needed to spray a little air freshener round to get rid of the lingering smell of curry and there was no trace that he had ever been there.

Callie wondered why she had felt the need to get rid of every last trace of him. Did she feel guilty? And if so, what for? She had done nothing wrong by anybody's standards. Or was she worried about Billy finding out and suspecting something? And if so, why? Not only was he the least jealous man she had ever met, she had only spent a pleasant evening with a friend and colleague, sharing a curry and a bottle of wine, or two. She checked the fridge; there was a little left in the second bottle, so it was only a bottle and a half between the two of them. But it did explain why she was a bit muzzy headed this morning.

Nothing that a cup of tea and some fresh air wouldn't clear, and perhaps it would also get rid of her nagging feeling of guilt. It had felt so natural, so comfortable, sitting on the sofa with Miller, sharing a meal. It had felt so right for him to be with her. Seeing him asleep, she had felt a rush of tenderness towards him and as she had tucked the blanket round him, she had a feeling that was almost like love.

But that didn't mean she had been unfaithful to Billy, she told herself as she wiped a smear of curry sauce off the printed-out patient records Miller had brought with him and put them into her bag. A last look around the room to make sure everything was in order and then she grabbed her umbrella and headed for the door. A brisk walk across the clifftop park would clear her head and banish these silly thoughts. It was just a shame that it was so cold, wet and windy.

* * *

She told herself that it wasn't just to reassure herself about her feelings for Billy that she dropped in to see him at lunchtime. Just as her decision not to update Miller in person about what was, or wasn't in the patient notes, but to do it by phone call wasn't because she was avoiding him. He'd been disappointed to hear that there was nothing suspicious in the notes. Callie had been right; there was no reason for either patient to have been given an intravenous drug, none had been ordered or prescribed by their doctors, nor had any blood tests been requested, and there was no record of any referrals to hospital. In short, there was absolutely no reason in the notes to explain the bruises and puncture marks found on the bodies. At least that pointed strongly to there being something for Miller to investigate, even though he hadn't sounded exactly pleased about it when she told him. But it had pleased her. It meant her instincts that this was foul

171

play had been right all along. And she couldn't wait to tell Billy.

"Hiya," she called out as she went into his office and gave him a kiss.

"What's got into you?" he asked, in surprise. She was normally far more reserved when they were both at work; something he had always found amusing.

"Oh, nothing," she said, "I just wanted to tell you how brilliant you are."

"Now I know something is up," he said with a laugh.

"I went through Elizabeth Mount's medical record and also that of Marek Bartosz. There were no reasonable or innocent explanations in there for them to have had any kind of IV intervention."

Billy smiled and heaved a sigh of relief that there was yet more supporting evidence that the two people had been murdered.

"Have you heard anything from Belfast? About the job?" she asked anxiously, still unsure that she wanted him to go but knowing how much it meant to him and to his future career.

"Not yet," he told her as he made them both coffee from his flash machine. "It's still very much on hold. They'll have heard that the second pathologist found cause for concern in both cases, but that's not exactly a complete vindication and I'm sure that Wadsworth will have been lobbying behind the scenes."

"Why?" She was appalled.

"If I'm right, he's wrong, and he is never, ever wrong," Billy told her.

"Well, he'll have to admit he's wrong when we catch the killer and they confess all."

He smiled again.

"That's why I love you." He hugged her. "You are the best and most optimistic person I know."

"Not to mention determined."

"I think you'll find that's stubborn actually," he told her with a smile and she hugged him back, but there was just a little bit of her, deep down, that felt ever so slightly guilty. Again.

* * *

Callie was looking forward to going home once evening surgery was finished. Billy had told her he would be coming round to cook a special meal, because even he could see that the weight of evidence was steadily tipping in his favour and maybe he hadn't lost his chance to become a Home Office pathologist after all. As he generally finished earlier than her, she knew he would already be at her home, getting everything ready. Callie just hoped it wasn't another curry, because she'd eaten quite enough the night before. Something healthier and less calorific might be in order, and maybe a bit less wine, but she wasn't hopeful she would be successful on either front. It was one thing to know what was good for you but quite another to actually do it and Callie knew that she would probably eat and drink too much again tonight. At least she would get some exercise afterwards and she could always find time to go to the gym tomorrow. Possibly.

As soon as her last patient had left, Callie picked up the telephone. She had been looking forward to making the call because it was nice when you had good news for a patient. Monica Claydon's test results were back and were showing a positive result for Lyme disease. It would be a while before they could be sure that the treatment she had started was the best one for her and that it was working, but Callie knew that most people felt better simply for knowing what was causing their problems, even if it was still likely to be a long haul back to fitness.

"Hello, Monica. It's Dr Hughes. I just wanted to tell you about your test results," Callie started to say once Monica had picked up.

Suddenly, there was the sound of shouting from the treatment room next door, and Callie hurriedly told Monica the good news and made sure that she had already started the antibiotics, trying to listen to what was going on outside at the same time.

"Oh, thank you so much, doctor. I can feel myself getting better already, just knowing what's making me so ill and knowing it can be treated. Thank you. Thank you so much."

Callie cut off her effusive thanks, said she would see her the following week to make sure she was improving and hurriedly said goodbye. The shouting was quieter now as if someone was trying to calm things down, but Callie still rushed out of her consulting room to see what was going on, almost knocking over the receptionist who was running along the corridor towards the noise as well. Raised voices were once again coming from the treatment room and both Callie and the receptionist stormed in, after only a cursory knock on the door, expecting to see the practice nurse being harangued by a patient.

"Don't you ever tell me what to do again! Ever! Do you hear me?"

A woman with her back to them shouted as they barged into the room. Mel, the nurse, was sitting at her desk, red in the face and tearful. She looked at them with relief and the woman shouting at her turned round, realising that she had an audience.

Both Callie and the receptionist stopped dead in their tracks. It was Eleanor who had been doing the shouting and she didn't seem pleased to see them. There was a moment of shocked silence before Callie recovered.

"What's going on?" she asked.

"This, this nurse" – Eleanor pointed at Mel and almost spat the word out – "deliberately undermined me by changing a patient's medication without even speaking to me first. She had no right to do that."

Callie looked at the tearful nurse for an explanation.

"Yes, but he couldn't manage—"

"You see?" Eleanor interrupted. "She admits it."

Callie turned to the receptionist.

"It's okay, I'll deal with this, you go and close up the surgery, make sure all the patients have left."

The receptionist seemed reluctant to go. This was much more interesting.

"Let's just everybody calm down and give me a chance to find out what's going on," Callie said firmly and ushered the receptionist out.

Once she had left, Callie pulled up a chair and indicated to Eleanor that she should as well.

"So, Mel, perhaps you can tell me what's happened?"

"Oh, I see, you're going to take her side, are you?" Eleanor complained.

"No. I'm just trying to find out the facts, from both of you, one at a time." Callie was determined not to be put off by Eleanor. "Now sit down and don't interrupt, you can tell me your side afterwards."

Eleanor didn't look happy, but she sat, nonetheless.

"Mr Miah is one of my asthma patients," Mel told her. "His peak flows were getting worse and when I saw him in clinic a few weeks ago, it was clear he really wasn't managing with standard inhalers, even with a spacer, so I spoke to Dr Grantham and we changed him to a dry powder device and it made a big difference."

Eleanor gave a derisive snort and Mel gave her a glare.

"Carry on, Mel," Callie said, holding up a hand to tell Eleanor to wait her turn.

"At the end of last week he rang me, said his asthma was getting worse and could he go back to the treatment I'd changed him to. I was a bit confused and asked him which treatment he was referring to and he explained that he'd seen Dr Sweeting when he needed a new prescription and she'd changed him back to his old inhalers. I thought it must have been a mistake."

She looked at Eleanor, who was staring out of the window, lips a thin line and arms tightly crossed.

"Anyway," Mel hurried on, "I went up to see Dr Sweeting and pointed out that we had changed Mr Miah to a new device and asked if she could do a new prescription."

"In front of Dr Grantham!" Eleanor hissed. "Can you believe it?"

"I'm sorry, perhaps I should have waited until you were alone, but I honestly thought it was just a simple mistake, that you hadn't realised it had been changed."

Callie was beginning to see what had happened. On top of everything else, having a nurse correct her in front of her tutor had been the final straw for Eleanor, even if the nurse was right.

"These things hap—" Callie started to say, trying to calm things down, before Eleanor interrupted.

"It wasn't a mistake. I deliberately changed him back to his old inhaler. There was no need for him to have the new device; he just needed to be given a spacer and be taught how to use it properly, and that's her job." Eleanor jerked a hand in Mel's direction. "Just because she doesn't want to take the time to teach him—"

"I tried. He just couldn't get the hang of it!" Mel looked as if she was about to explode. "He's an old man and learning how to use these things was beyond him."

"Do you know how much one of the devices you put him on costs?"

"Less than an admission for poorly controlled asthma," Callie cut in firmly before Mel could say anything back. "Now, please, let's just calm down."

To her relief, both Mel and Eleanor kept quiet.

"Eleanor, Mel is a highly-trained asthma nurse and if she says the best device for Mr Miah is the one she suggested, then it is."

"But—"

"As you pointed out, she is the one who spends the time teaching the patients how to use their devices, which is, after all, what we pay her to do and we all trust her to tell us what suits them best."

Mel chose the wrong moment to give Eleanor a smug little smile on hearing herself described as an expert.

"She's just a nurse!" Eleanor exploded. "And I am a doctor! And if I say a patient should have a cheaper device, because these expensive ones are just a waste of precious money then that's what he should have!"

Eleanor stood abruptly and stormed out of the room, slamming the door behind her.

Callie could hear her all the way down the corridor and leaving the building. Callie looked at Mel who heaved a sigh of relief.

"I'm sorry about that, Mel. I'll have a chat with her and Dr Grantham in the morning. Don't worry about it. Why don't you get off home now?"

Mel nodded.

"Thanks, Callie, I'll just finish clearing up and I'll be off." She hesitated before adding, "I've never been spoken to like that, ever, and you need to know I won't put up with it again."

"I don't blame you."

Callie left her to it.

On her way up to the office she checked to see if Dr Grantham was in his room. But he had left. However, Linda, the practice manager, was waiting for her in the office.

"What was all that about?" she asked. "I heard Eleanor reduced Mel to tears."

"It was just another hissy fit," was Callie's explanation. There was no point playing it down or trying to sugar-coat it; Callie knew that Linda would have to deal with the aftermath from the nurses, not to mention the gossip among the receptionists. "She was very rude to Mel, and she had no cause to be."

"Even if she did have cause, she should have come to you or Dr Grantham."

"I agree. Look, I'll have a word with Dr Grantham tomorrow and get him to speak to her."

"If she comes in tomorrow," Linda said.

"Indeed, if she comes in. Well, if she doesn't…" Callie shrugged, "…then that will be another black mark, and she might well lose her place on the training programme."

* * *

"I just don't understand why she would be like that," Callie told Billy later, as they ate Thai green curry that Billy had ready for her when she finally got back from the surgery. "I mean, to speak to a colleague in that way, any colleague, let alone someone like Mel. She was totally out of order. I really think Dr Grantham will kick her out tomorrow and to lose two training places is unheard of. Nowhere else is likely to take her on."

"And that's as it should be." Billy was unsympathetic. "I mean, would you really want someone like that to be your GP?"

He had a point.

"Come on." He refilled her glass. "Let's forget about her and enjoy this evening."

Callie was busy trying to ignore just how many calories she must be eating. She took a large sip of the delicious, cold, wine, forgetting her earlier good intentions, and concentrated on trying to put the scene with Eleanor out of her mind, but it was easier said than done. She had been so convinced that the trainee had been unfairly treated at her last training practice, bullied even, and yet it was becoming increasingly obvious that Dr Richardson might not be the one at fault. Eleanor's poor temper control and her fragile ego meant that any attempt to correct her decisions, or just suggest better ways of handling things, seemed to lead to resentment, sulking and now even worse behaviour. It meant that she was impossible to teach. How could she learn the right way to do things, if she wouldn't let anyone tell her what they were?

"It will be interesting to see if she turns up to work tomorrow," Billy added, realising that he still didn't have her full attention.

"Actually, it's her study day."

"Maybe that's a good thing. Gives her time to cool off."

"You could be right." Callie thought for a moment. "Or she could just sulk all day and be even more resentful when she comes back."

Callie knew which of the scenarios her money was on; Eleanor had shown she didn't forget slights against her easily, no matter whether they were real slights or imagined.

# Chapter 25

Having carefully arrived only just in time for her morning surgery, Callie spent most of rest of the session trying to avoid her colleagues and thereby the need to say anything about the incident of the night before. It was clearly the main item of gossip amongst the office staff and receptionists, who seemed to have built it up into a major incident. In a way it was, she supposed. Callie was sure that Linda would have said something to Dr Grantham by now as well, and she half-expected to be called into his room for a meeting to discuss the trainee's future, or lack of it. With that in mind, she kept up with as much of the paperwork as possible as she went along, and as soon as her last patient had gone out of the door, grabbed her bag and did the same. Heaving a sigh of relief that she had got out of the surgery without being summoned, she set off, at a brisk pace, along the seafront.

The fresh sea air and the sight of the fishing boats pulled up on the beach never failed to lighten her mood and she found herself a dry place to sit and look at the waves while eating the sandwich she had picked up from the café next door to the surgery. She needed time to think. She really wasn't sure what should be done with regard to Eleanor. Not that it was entirely her decision, but she knew that Dr Grantham would give weight to her opinion, and she didn't want to make any rash judgements. She really didn't want to end the woman's career unless she was absolutely sure that was needed.

She had to admit that Billy was probably right to say that Eleanor wasn't suited to being a GP, given the two incidents with Monica and Mel. And what if there had been more events that she didn't know about? Maybe at her previous practice?

Aware that a hungry seagull, who had been eyeing her sandwich for some time, was getting braver, and closer, by the minute, and that there seemed to be a few of his mates circling overhead, Callie threw him the last of her lunch and stood up. A crowd of seagulls descended on the crusts, fighting over every crumb, and Callie was pleased to see the bird she had thrown the scraps to seemed to have come out of the scrum with a large chunk of bread in his beak.

Callie brushed herself down. She had come to a decision. She needed to talk to Dr Richardson about Eleanor and get his view before she spoke to Dr Grantham and any irrevocable action was taken. She just hoped he was still at his surgery and not out doing visits already.

* * *

"It's a delicate matter," she said into her phone as she walked briskly towards the town centre where Dr Richardson had his practice. "I think it would be best if I spoke to you face-to-face. I'm only about five minutes away." Well, five minutes if she broke into a run, she corrected herself silently, increasing her pace as she did so.

She was surprised when he agreed to see her, albeit reluctantly, and said he would wait in reception. Provided he didn't have to wait long.

As she arrived there, a little out of breath, Dr Richardson was standing by the door, impatiently glancing at his watch. He quickly ushered her into his consulting room. He probably didn't want anyone to see them, she thought, and perhaps he was right to be cautious. Neither of them would want this meeting getting back to Eleanor in her current mood.

"Giving you a headache, is she?" he asked once the door was closed.

"Um, just a bit," she admitted.

"I tried to warn Hugh Grantham about her when he suggested she move practices, but not to put too fine a point on it, I was glad for her to leave us, so I may not have tried very hard."

"Why did you want her to go?"

"I really didn't want to get any more complaints."

"From patients?"

"Patients, staff, but mostly from Eleanor herself. She seemed to have an endless list of grievances against everybody, including myself."

Callie nodded. It fitted with how things had been at her own surgery. She could kick herself for not having seen it sooner.

"Do you have any specific incidents you can tell me about? Particularly with regard to patients?" If upsetting or irritating your colleagues was grounds for sacking, a lot of doctors would be out of jobs, Callie knew. He hesitated.

"Nothing official, but just for me to be sure, in my own mind, about any action that needs to be taken," Callie reassured him.

"Okay, so, she upset an obese patient by telling her she was a burden on the NHS."

"Oh dear."

"And then there was the injured rugger player; she said it was a self-inflicted injury and he ought to have it fixed privately – oh, and there was the old lady she told that it

182

wasn't worth referring her for a new heart valve because she wouldn't live long enough to make it worthwhile."

When he finally paused for breath, Callie gave a sigh.

"I think we have to accept that she's probably not suited to being a GP," she said.

"No, and not when she can't take criticism, no matter how gently put and constructive it is," he said with feeling. "You have to wonder if she's suited to a career in medicine at all."

Once they had talked about the trainee a bit more and both recounted some more incidents they had witnessed, Callie took a quick look at her watch.

"I'm going to have to go, if I'm to do my visits and get back in time for evening surgery," she said as she stood up.

"Of course, and good luck with our Dr Sweeting. I hope you get it all sorted." He stood as well and opened the door. "Oh, and what happened about our patient? The one who fitted with your scenario – you know, found sitting in a chair as if she was about to go on holiday?" he asked as they walked towards the surgery entrance.

"We've discounted her because some aspects didn't fit," Callie told him. "Her niece said she really was going on holiday the day she died, so the police are not looking into it."

She gave him a brief wave before hurrying away. It wasn't until she was almost back at her own workplace that she realised that he hadn't looked pleased or relieved by the news. In fact, he had looked decidedly puzzled, but she put it out of her mind as she steeled herself; she was going to have to talk to Dr Grantham. Her mind was made up, and now it was time for him to make a decision too.

# Chapter 26

When Callie walked back to her flat that night, her head was full of the conversation she had had with Dr Grantham before leaving work. A decision had been made to terminate Eleanor Sweeting's training contract with them. As it was not a day Eleanor was in the surgery, Dr Grantham was calling her to explain that they were concerned about her suitability, and that she should not come in until he had spoken to the training department. Callie suspected that Eleanor wouldn't take it well.

Going into her flat, she saw that the light was blinking on the answer machine, which reminded her that she hadn't switched her phone back on to ring after surgery. She always put it on silent rather than vibrate so that she wouldn't be distracted whilst talking to patients, even by the buzzing. She clicked the television on to catch the end of the local news and pulled her mobile phone from her bag, switching it on and putting it on the countertop, then reaching for a glass from the cupboard.

"A reminder of our top news of the day—" the news presenter was saying as Callie opened the fridge and pulled out the almost empty bottle of wine. She looked up and was startled to see a harassed looking Miller on the television, trying to push his way past a group of reporters outside the police station, and saying, "No comment," repeatedly.

She was momentarily distracted by her mobile phone buzzing and she picked it up as the presenter continued:

"Police have refused to confirm or deny that pensioners in the East Sussex town of Hastings are being targeted by a serial killer but a source has told us that several old people have died in suspicious circumstances and warned that people should take care never to let anyone they don't know into their homes. Take care, and goodnight."

Callie was stunned. She had thought that perhaps some publicity might help stop future attacks, but understood when Miller had said they had to be sure someone really was killing off old people before spreading alarm and panic to such a vulnerable group. Had he changed his mind, or had someone in his team taken it upon themselves to do it for him?

She poured herself a glass of wine and picked up her phone. She was surprised to see that she had twenty-five missed calls and ten messages and then her phone started ringing again. It was Miller.

"Hello," she answered. "I've just—"

"Why on earth did you go and talk to a bloody reporter?" he cut in angrily, not even giving her a chance to finish her sentence. He sounded furious.

"I didn't," she responded coldly, stopping him in his tracks.

"Who else could it be?" he asked, slightly less angrily. "You were the one who wanted them involved."

"Yes, but I would never go to them behind your back. Not under any circumstances." She crossed her fingers thinking that there were indeed several circumstances where she might consider doing just that. "And I promise that I didn't this time. I take it that the press won't tell you who their source is?"

"No." He snorted at the thought and then sighed. She could almost see him, running his hands through his hair, making it stand up in tufts, and the thought made her smile.

"Have you thought about whether or not one of your team might have leaked the story?"

"If they have, they'll be out on their ear," he said, "but to be honest, they all know it's too early to say for sure that we do have a serial killer as opposed to, oh, I don't know, a couple of cases of manslaughter, or medical negligence."

"I agree."

"Really?"

"That you were right, it is too early to go to the press, although I can't pretend that I'm not pleased that they know now. I mean, I'm convinced there is a killer and this is going to make their job a whole lot harder. If they plan on killing anyone else, that is."

"True," he conceded.

"I missed the full report. Did the press mention that the people who died were found looking as if they were going away?"

"Yes," he replied. "They described the scenes at the beginning and said that we had had four deaths."

"Four?"

"Yes, exactly," he replied. "Four, although we're actually only investigating two, as you know and disagree with, as you think there may have been three, which is why I thought that it must have been you who spoke to the press."

"But why would I have said four?" She thought about that for a moment. "Who else knew about Mr Bartosz?"

"The coroner, of course, and the mortuary bods, the pathologists and staff." He paused as he thought some more. "And didn't you raise it with the GPs at that meeting?"

"No," she said. "I only told them about the two cases, not Mr Bartosz as he didn't die until after that meeting, so the two GPs who reported the original cases and all the people there would only say that there were two."

"But a third was brought up by someone there?"

"Not until after the meeting and we discounted that one because she really was going on holiday." As she said that, Dr Richardson's puzzled face came to her but her thought process was interrupted by her home phone ringing.

"Look, I've got to go, but I promise, it wasn't me who spoke to the press," and she finished the call, hoping that he believed her. He had seemed to.

"Hi," she said picking up the home phone having checked who it was.

"Did you see the news?" Billy said excitedly. "Miller didn't look happy."

"I know, I've already spoken to him. He seemed to think I was the source."

"I'm taking it you weren't?"

"Of course not! Believe me, I'd have warned you if I was going to do something like that. Have the press been onto you?"

"Yup, they have. Repeatedly. I've told the switchboard not to put any more calls through to the mortuary. Fortunately, they don't seem to have got hold of my personal number yet."

"Let me warn you that Miller's going to be looking for whoever was the source of the leak, so he'll be wanting to question you and Jim."

"I know, he's already rung me and someone's going to come and speak to Jim tomorrow, but I'm confident it can't be him, not least because he only knew about the two cases and they talked about four on the telly. Who do you think the fourth case is?"

"No idea. It's strange, isn't it? The only people who are pretty sure there are more than two cases are you, me,

Mike, the coroner and the police and we all think there are three."

"There's the killer of course. They would know how many they had killed."

"Yes, but it's not in their best interest to tell everyone about it, is it?"

"Notoriety," Billy said confidently. "They want the world to know just how clever they are."

But somehow, Callie didn't think that fitted her impression of the killer. It was a problem that continued to nag at her throughout the evening.

# Chapter 27

Callie wasn't surprised to find Miller waiting for her when she arrived at the surgery the next morning. She had had to turn off her home phone because of the huge number of calls she was getting from reporters, both local and national, and she had put her mobile on silent overnight so that she could at least try and sleep. When she had switched it on and checked it in the morning, there had been far too many calls and messages and too little time for her to try and answer them.

Unfortunately, the night before, despite the silent phone, her brain hadn't played ball with the idea of sleep and she had lain awake, wrestling with the conundrum of why the reporters believed there were four deaths, rather than just the two being investigated by the police. Everyone had been so careful not to add Alan Darling, Caroline Stratton's patient and the likely first victim, to the list because he was not only dead and buried, so to speak, but cremated into the bargain. They would never know if he was a victim, despite evidence to suggest that he might have been. So, only two deaths were being investigated: Mrs Mount and Mr Bartosz.

When she spoke at the LMC meeting, of course, she had counted Mr Darling then, giving her two deaths with Mrs Mount again. June Dingwell, Dr Richardson's patient, was only being added, and removed again, afterwards.

And who knew about Mr Bartosz? Only the nurses along with his doctor and maybe the management team at Hastings Care. She had rung Amanda Ayling first thing and asked her about that, careful not to accuse anyone of having spoken to the press, and Amanda had said she would look into it. She had sounded harassed and Callie could only wonder at the stress she must be under with the press and the problems with her staff.

Callie ushered Miller into the consulting room and wasn't surprised to hear a knock at the door almost before she had managed to sit down.

"I've brought coffee," Linda said as she came in, with a laden tray.

"Thanks, Linda. That's very kind of you."

Callie tried to suppress a smile as Linda dithered in the doorway, clearly wanting to know what was going on; bringing the coffee had simply been a ruse to get into the room.

There were a couple of moments' silence before Linda took the hint and left, but Callie was pretty sure she was still in the corridor hoping to hear what was said. Unfortunately for her, the walls and door were well soundproofed as they needed to protect patient confidentiality, so Callie doubted she would be able to hear much unless they shouted. There was no real need for Linda to try and listen in, anyway, because she would get it all out of Callie later. She had her ways.

Callie turned her attention to Miller and thought how tired he looked. If the pressure to solve this had been there before, it must be much worse now that word was out.

"Have you managed to find out who the source of the information is yet?" she asked.

He shook his head.

"It's been driving me crazy," he admitted. "Trying to work out who knew what. And where four has come from."

"Me too," she replied. "I've put some feelers out amongst the doctors and with the care team, but—" she was interrupted by her mobile ringing. She picked it up and saw that it was Amanda from Hastings Care. "Excuse me a minute," she said to Miller. "I should take this."

She went out into the corridor and was unsurprised to see Linda hovering by the front desk. She turned and walked away from the waiting room as she answered the call; she didn't know how Amanda's employers would feel about her involvement and she didn't want to get Amanda into trouble for speaking to her.

"Hi, Amanda," she said. From the background traffic noise she could hear down the line, it sounded as if Amanda was also out of the office, most likely in the car park. "Have you got any information for me?"

"Not about who has spoken to the reporters, I'm afraid, but several of the nurses have told me that Dr Richardson has been asking them questions about another patient who died a while ago."

"Mrs Dingwell?"

"You know about her and about how she was found?"

"Well, yes, but we discounted her because she really was going on holiday. I told Dr Richardson."

Callie remembered how puzzled he had looked when she had told the doctor that.

"Really? Well, he doesn't seem to have accepted it. He is definitely still thinking that she might be another one. Oh, and one other thing," she added, "I thought I'd let you know that Trudy Wells has been admitted for rehab. A place up in the Lake District, miles from anywhere. Her manager got her in there, insisted she go or else he was going to get HR involved, but he didn't want to say anything to you or anyone else because of confidentiality."

"When did she go?"

"Last Thursday."

The day after Mr Bartosz had died and the nurse had failed to turn up to see her later patients. Had she killed him before going away?

Callie thanked Amanda and, having got details of where the rehab centre was, went back into her consulting room.

"Anything helpful?" Miller asked her hopefully as she came in.

"I don't honestly know," she told him, and explained about Dr Richardson still believing that Mrs Dingwell should be part of the investigation. "And he was Mr Bartosz's GP, or it was his practice anyway. So, if he really does think she's still a possible victim, even if we know she isn't, then that would explain the four victims' angle."

"You think he went to the press?"

"It's the only explanation that fits."

"He's probably on the phone to some reporter or other as we speak." Miller took a deep breath and stood up. "Right, it would help me if I knew for sure. And give me the pleasure of informing the Chief that it wasn't one of us."

Callie could imagine that the Chief Superintendent would also be mightily relieved that it wasn't one of his officers who had spoken to the press.

"Which surgery does this Dr Richardson work at?"

Miller looked almost chirpy as he hurried out with the information, intent on clearing his team, Callie, and himself, from blame.

Callie, for her own part, wondered why on earth Dr Richardson thought that June Dingwell was one of the victims, despite Callie's assurance that she wasn't. So sure of it, in fact, that he had gone to the press when he thought that Callie and the police had dismissed the idea and were not investigating the deaths with the intensity that he thought was needed.

* * *

Monica almost bounced into Callie's consulting room.

"Wow!" Callie said to her.

"I know, I feel so much better, doctor," she said. "Oh, don't worry, I know it's going to take time to really get back to normal, but I'm just so happy that things are definitely moving in the right direction. You've no idea what a difference that makes."

Callie couldn't stop herself from smiling when she thought of how improved her patient seemed, even much later when she was up in the main doctor's office. If Dr Grantham was surprised that she smiled when he told her that the regional training team had been very disappointed to hear he was terminating Eleanor's training contract, he didn't say anything.

"Their reaction is understandable," she told him.

"Yes, I know that it reflects badly on them as well as Eleanor." He seemed more upset by this than by her poor performance. "They tried very hard to get me to change my mind, but I refused, even when they hinted that they wouldn't send anyone to the practice again."

"They wouldn't do that," Callie tried to reassure him. "They are always desperate for places for their trainees."

He accepted her reassurance, but when she continued to smile as she tackled her emails, she had to explain to her colleagues why she was so cheerful.

"It's wonderful, isn't it? When you actually help someone like that. You should be proud," Gauri Sinha, one of her colleagues at the practice, told her when she explained about Monica. And that's exactly how she felt, proud. So often her work meant just trying to ease things, slow down disease progression; it was rarely quite so transformative.

"By the way," Gauri continued, "you know you talked about the old people being found? Asked if we knew of any vulnerable patients planning a holiday all of a sudden?"

Callie looked up from her computer, suddenly very interested.

"Yes?"

"My patient, Mrs Friend, eighty-five, bit confused, well, very confused. Last week, Friday, when I went to visit, she said that she wouldn't need me to come this week, I usually go and see her as often as I can, you see," she explained, and Callie had to stop herself from telling Gauri to hurry up and get to the point. "Well, she told me that I didn't need to go this Friday as she would be away. I didn't think anything about it at the time, I assumed she was going into respite or something, but with what was on the news last night, it reminded me and I thought—"

She seemed surprised to see Callie rushing for the door.

# Chapter 28

Callie looked up the details of Mrs Dorothy Friend, generally known as Dolly, from the records and called her straight away.

"Hello? Mrs Friend? This is the surgery calling."

"The who?"

"The surgery. The doctor."

"I don't need a doctor."

"No, I know, it's just that we heard you were going away."

"Pardon? You'll have to speak up dear, I'm a little deaf."

"Are you going on holiday, Mrs Friend?" she shouted into the phone, aware that she had the whole office's attention now.

"Am I going where?"

"Are you going on holiday?"

"I'm sorry, dear, it's very nice of you to call for a chat but I can't talk now, I'm very busy, I'm going away. Goodbye."

"No! Don't—"

But she had already put the phone down.

"Call the police, get them to go round there, say it's an emergency," she said to Linda as she headed for the door.

She called Miller as she raced up the stairs to the top of the East Cliff, not wanting to wait for the lift.

"Hi, Steve? I'm on my way to visit a Mrs Friend at 43a Whiteleas Estate. She is supposed to be going away on holiday this week. I called her but she said she was going away and put the phone down."

"Does her profile fit with the others?"

"Yes, she's in her eighties, vulnerable and confused."

Callie was puffing as she reached the top of the steps and headed across the country park to her home and her car. She really needed to spend more time at the gym.

"It's a Tuesday, though. Mr Bartosz was killed on a Wednesday."

"But the others were on a Tuesday. Mr Bartosz could have been the odd one out."

"And the nurse is in rehab up north, isn't she?"

"Yes, but we don't know it's her, do we? I mean, it might be but what if I'm wrong?"

That seemed to convince him.

"I'll get a patrol car there straight away."

"Hopefully one's already going there, I asked the surgery to call the emergency number."

"I'll check, but don't go in until they are there, please."

She could hear that he was already hurrying to get there too.

* * *

By the time Callie arrived at the address, there was already a patrol car parked outside the ground-floor flat. A paved area in front of the living room windows sported a variety of gnomes, windmills and mismatched pots of dead plants. Callie rang from the main entrance to the building and, having identified herself to the policeman who answered, was buzzed in. By the time she reached the front door, it was already open and a policeman that Callie recognised but couldn't put a name to was looking relieved to see her.

"Hi, I'm—" she started to introduce herself.

"Come in, doctor," he cut in without letting her finish and stepped back to allow her to pass. "Back room, straight ahead."

Slightly apprehensive as to what she might find when she entered the room, Callie was relieved to see Dolly Friend sitting on a very elderly pink velour sofa, and she wasn't looking particularly pleased to see them. A female police officer Callie knew was sitting in one of the matching armchairs and they both looked up as Callie came into the room.

"Good to see you, Dr Hughes," Abi Adeola, the police officer, said with a welcoming smile, before turning to the old lady and saying loudly, "The doctor's here to see you. Shall I go and make a cup of tea?"

"Thank you, dear, but I must get on." She looked at Callie. "I didn't call the doctor."

"No, but I just wanted to make sure you were all right."

"Why wouldn't I be?"

Mrs Friend seemed a little irritated by what was going on, but Callie took no notice and sat down as Abi left, presumably also ignoring her and going to the kitchen to make the tea. Callie took a closer look at the elderly woman. Her cardigan was buttoned incorrectly but otherwise, she looked clean and well-cared for.

"What is it you need to do, Mrs Friend?" Callie asked.

"Um, lots of things."

She looked around her for some clue as to what exactly it was she was supposed to be doing. There was a suitcase, open, on an upright dining chair next to a small drop-leaf table. The case seemed to contain a random collection of items, a pair of shoes, a bar of soap and a garden ornament, but when Mrs Friend saw it, her face brightened immediately.

"Pack! That's it." She turned to Callie. "I'm going away, you know."

"How lovely," Callie smiled encouragingly. "Where are you going?"

Mrs Friend thought for a moment, looked out of the window and then down at her pink slippers before coming out with what she hoped was a good answer.

"Somewhere nice. Very nice indeed."

"How exciting. Are you going with anyone?"

"Yes, my carer. She's a lovely girl."

"Your carer's taking you away? That's kind of her."

Callie was aware that Miller had come into the room and was standing quietly by the door, listening to the conversation.

"She's a nice girl," she repeated before fixing a beady eye on Miller. "Do I know you?"

Miller was still thinking of a suitable reply when she continued before he could answer.

"Of course! You're Benita's boy, aren't you? She said you were coming. Come and have a seat and tell me how your mother is." She patted the seat next to her and Miller reluctantly came forward.

"Erm, I don't think—" he started to say, but Callie decided to ignore Mrs Friend's conversation with him and continue to ask her questions.

"Are you expecting her today?"

"Who?"

"Your carer."

"Now that depends on what day it is, doesn't it?" Mrs Friend answered with impeccable logic. She seemed to have forgotten Miller, who, Callie was pleased to note, had moved as far away as he possibly could while remaining in the room and was trying to keep as still as possible. She was also pleased to see that he had also stopped Abi from coming in with the tea. She didn't want anything to distract Mrs Friend.

"Today is Tuesday. Does she come on a Tuesday?" Callie continued to gently probe.

"Now you're trying to catch me out, aren't you?" Mrs Friend gave a little smile. "She used to come on a Tuesday but now she comes on a Wednesday." She seemed very pleased with herself for not falling for what she thought was a trick question.

"You're not expecting her today?"

"Not today, no. Not if it's Tuesday today." She looked at Callie to check that she'd got that right and Callie gave her a little nod of encouragement. "It's Wednesday she comes. Tomorrow," Mrs Friend explained patiently. "She said she was coming tomorrow and I had to be all packed and ready."

"And can you tell me what her name is?"

"Who?"

"Your carer." If Callie felt this conversation was a little repetitive, she was taking care not to show it.

"Of course."

"And?"

Mrs Friend looked puzzled.

"Your carer's name is?" Callie prompted her, knowing that people with dementia, or even benign forgetfulness, would often try to hide the fact that they had forgotten something like the name of a person or object but it was hard to do that if you were asked a direct question.

"You know, what's-her-name?" Mrs Friend gesticulated with her hand, clearly frustrated by her inability to remember, and the fact that none of them could help her.

"Is her name Benita?" Callie tried.

"Of course not." Mrs Friend laughed at the idea. "I was at school with Benita. She can barely care for herself, let alone anyone else."

"So, what is your carer's name?"

Callie and Miller waited patiently, but Mrs Friend clearly wasn't going to remember anytime soon, so Callie tried a different tack.

"Is your carer from Hastings Care?" she asked.

"No, definitely not," she said, with a dismissive wave of her hand. "They just come to get me up and give me my tablets. Never have time for a chat, they don't. Not like Dr Sinha. She comes once a week. She's a nice lady. Doesn't rush me."

"She is nice, isn't she," Callie said with a smile. "And is Dr Sinha the only person who comes to visit you?"

"No, no, I get lots of visits." Mrs Friend paused as if she was about to come out with a list, but then realised that there weren't really that many people. Not that she could remember, anyway. "My family have all gone. Moved away. Don't see any of them anymore," she said sadly.

"So just Dr Sinha?" Callie prompted.

"Just her and the other one."

"The other one?" Callie tried again.

"Yes. Her." Mrs Friend still couldn't seem to remember the name. "From that, that place. The, um, cha—" Mrs Friend stopped what she was saying suddenly and closed her mouth firmly.

"From the charity?"

"No, not from any charity." She said quickly and gave Callie a sly look. "Not from there. Definitely not from there." She paused and gave a theatrical yawn. "I'm a bit tired now, dear," she said and closed her eyes. She was clearly not going to answer any more questions.

Callie decided it was probably best to let her have a rest and that maybe she would be more help after a nap, so she and Miller joined the two constables in the small kitchen.

"We can't leave her here on her own," Callie said. "Just in case this carer comes."

"She's not due until tomorrow."

"I know, but what if she comes early, or Mrs Friend has got the day wrong. We can't risk it."

"What do you suggest we do?" he asked her. "Can you put her in a home or something?"

"It's not that easy," Callie explained. "There aren't spare places readily available and respite care has a waiting list as long as your arm."

"A relative?" he said hopefully.

"You heard her, Steve, they've all gone or moved away. I'll check with the surgery, but I'm not hopeful." She sighed. "Don't you have a safe house or something?"

He laughed at the idea.

"Don't you have a volunteer group, you know: 'Friends of the Surgery' type of thing?"

"No, but actually," she conceded, "that's not such a bad idea. There's the Ada Holmes Charity."

"The one you tried to infiltrate using your mother?" He laughed and Callie could see Abi grinning too. She suspected the whole station knew about her mother's theatrics. "I assume they provide carers."

"Well, yes, they do – well, helpers more than carers – and I thought she was going to say this woman came from them, but then she seemed to clam up."

"I noticed that too, but she seemed adamant that this woman wasn't from a charity."

Callie wasn't convinced.

"We've already established that they weren't involved with Mr Bartosz, haven't we?" she checked.

"There's been no mention of them," he told her, but that wasn't the same thing at all. She tried to think of another solution, but couldn't, there was nobody she could think of who would be able to do it.

"Maybe they might be able to provide someone to come and stay here. To be honest, it's our only hope." She gave Miller a firm look, "And no, I'm not going to move in, even just for a day or so. But I am still a little bit worried about it, in case."

"Okay," he said with a smile, "well why don't we go and see them? Then we can make sure this mysterious carer who definitely doesn't come from any charity according to Mrs Friend, really doesn't come from them.

Then, if you are reassured, we can try and get them to provide someone to stay with Mrs Friend for a day or two."

Callie had to admit that seemed like a sensible course of action.

"And meanwhile?"

"And meanwhile, perhaps Constable Adeola here could stay?" He looked at the constable.

"I can stay as long as the Sarge can spare me," she replied amiably.

"You'll let us know if you get called away?" Callie asked her anxiously, not wanting Mrs Friend to be suddenly left on her own.

"Of course. And if she remembers who her mysterious carer is or where she is from, I'll give you a call, too."

"Great."

It seemed the best that anyone could do, so they left her to it.

Callie and Miller parted on the doorstep to go to their respective cars and agreed to meet at the charity offices.

As she hurried to where she had parked, Callie phoned the surgery. Linda picked up the call and gave a long, loud sigh.

"It's okay, I've already cancelled your afternoon visits. Am I going to have to move your evening patients as well?"

Callie reassured her that she still expected to be back in time for the evening surgery and ended the call.

Just as she reached the place where she had parked, she saw a figure out of the corner of her eye on the other side of the road. Callie stopped to get a better look as the woman hurried along the road, head turned away as if she was checking the houses as she walked. She was wearing a raincoat with the hood up despite it being a warm and dry day, and Callie could not see her face at all. Then she turned down an alleyway between the houses and was quickly out of sight.

Callie shivered despite the warmth of the sun. There was something about the way the woman had moved that had seemed furtive and out of place.

Even though the killer wasn't expected until tomorrow, she wondered if she could possibly have just seen her.

# Chapter 29

The charity shop didn't seem to have changed much since Callie's last visit. Exactly the same clothes and knick-knacks were in the window along with a growing amount of dust and cobwebs.

As she approached the counter with Miller, Callie asked for Joyce, the manager she had met on her earlier visit. As before, she was directed upstairs after a brief phone call. Miller followed her as they made their way to the back corridor, weaving between rubbish sacks filled to overflowing with clothes and toys.

"What are you going to say to her?" he asked in a whisper.

Callie had thought about how she was going to explain her change of role to the charity manager and had decided that honesty was the best policy. In fact, it was probably the only policy. Joyce was unlikely to be happy that she had been lied to before and nothing Callie said could change the fact that she had, but hopefully the manager would understand that Callie's intentions had been good. Callie also hoped she wouldn't take offence at them asking questions that might well lead her to understand that her volunteers were under suspicion.

As they went into the messy office where Joyce was sitting at her cluttered desk, she looked up. She was once again dressed in a rather eclectic outfit that featured animal prints and chunky costume jewellery in a variety of bright colours. Her reading glasses hung from a sizeable gold-coloured chain around her neck. Understandably, Joyce looked surprised to see Callie.

"Miss Hughes? Have you changed your mind? I'm sure I can persuade Derek to help with your mother if so. He was quite taken with her." Joyce brushed a wayward strand of hair from her face and tucked it under one of the many combs that were not doing a good job of controlling her hair.

"No, no. My mother is fine, thank you. In fact, I have a confession to make." Callie did her best not to look at Miller while she explained and apologised for her previous deception, but she could imagine his expression, nonetheless. Once she had finished her story, which she managed without any interruptions, she concluded by saying that she was actually now at the office in an official capacity, and then introduced Miller as well.

To be fair, after the initial confusion, Joyce quickly understood what Callie had done, and accepted the situation with good grace.

"I can't say that I'm pleased about it," she told Callie. "But what can I do to help now?"

Callie heaved a sigh of relief. She had half-expected to be thrown out, and she wouldn't have blamed the manager if she had been.

Miller took over the conversation at this point.

"We are investigating two suspicious deaths of elderly people in the locality and as your charity is connected to at least one of them, I wanted to ask you some questions and see if you have any information that might assist us."

"Of course, I saw it on the news. So awful. I'll try and help you in any way that I can."

"Can I ask if anyone from here visits a Mrs Friend?"

"Dolly Friend? Yes and no." Joyce seemed understandably hesitant to give them any details. After weighing it up, she continued. "She was one of ours, but she cancelled a week or two ago. Please tell me she hasn't come to any harm?"

"She's fine," Miller reassured her, and said nothing more.

"Then why are you asking about her?"

"Because of an incident that might be connected."

Callie wanted to give her enough information to get her talking without revealing anything confidential.

"I have to tell you I was rather concerned about her cancelling our visitor because I didn't like to leave her without any help. Oh," – Joyce waved her hand dismissively – "I know that she had carers coming in most days, but they are in and out so fast. It's not like having someone sit and take time to make sure that you are really all right, is it?"

Callie had to agree.

"Do you know why she cancelled?"

"No, I tried to get her to tell me but she can be quite hard to pin down to exact statements, you know?"

Callie and Miller did know, all too well.

"It's because of the dementia," Joyce continued. "They will try and cover for the fact that they have forgotten an answer by changing the subject or simply ignoring the question."

That described the situation with Mrs Friend perfectly, Callie thought.

"Can I just ask if you had any dealings with any of the following people?" Miller asked and when Joyce nodded her acquiescence went on to ask about Alan Darling, Elizabeth Mount and Marek Bartosz.

"Yes, we had a call from the police about Mr Bartosz already, but we definitely haven't had anything to do with him – but the other two, we did. They were both on our visit list."

"The same visitor?" Miller asked.

"Let me check." Joyce pulled up a spreadsheet on her computer. "No, different ones." She seemed about to say more, but then thought better of it.

"And June Dingwell?" Callie threw in, in desperation, even though they were no longer linking her to the others.

"That name doesn't ring a bell." Joyce checked the list. "No, we've never visited her."

"Would you be willing to let us have a list of your volunteers?" Miller asked.

"For what reason?"

"So that we can eliminate them from our enquiries."

She didn't answer immediately.

"Hmm. I'm not sure I can do that for a number of reasons from confidentiality to data protection," she explained and took off her reading glasses and let them dangle. "It's hard enough getting volunteers without them believing I've handed their details over to a third party. Tell me, Detective Inspector, do you really suspect that one of our volunteers might be going round killing off old people? I mean, it really is quite ridiculous, if you don't mind me saying so. Most of the people we accept as visitors have already cared for their own loved ones with dementia, and I can assure you they have all been vetted."

"If you think about it, going round killing old people at all is really quite ridiculous," Miller told her.

"Beyond our imagination," Callie added. "Well, beyond mine, anyway."

"But you must understand that we need to follow up every connection, no matter how bizarre," Miller added and Joyce nodded an acknowledgement.

"Of course. I'll think about it. Get advice even," she told him. "Do you think we should do anything more?" she asked. "Warn our clients, perhaps?"

"I wouldn't want to alarm anyone, or cause panic unnecessarily," Miller said, "but perhaps a general reminder to be careful would be in order."

"And maybe," Callie suggested, "your volunteers could do visits in pairs, wherever possible?"

The look on Joyce's face told her that the request was probably not going to be possible and Callie could understand it. The charity had limited numbers of volunteers and were almost certainly already stretched to their limit.

\* \* \*

"Visit in pairs?" Miller queried as they walked back to where their cars were parked sometime later. "Are you still thinking they might be involved?"

"Not really," she admitted, "but it doesn't hurt to be careful and by going to do visits together it will protect both their clients and the volunteers. And she did agree to try and do it."

"I can't see them keeping it up for long, though," Miller added, and Callie had to agree. What with Derek having agreed to go and stay with Mrs Friend, along with Joyce herself, for the next day or so, it must have left them extremely short-handed. "What next?" he asked her as they reached her blue Audi TT.

"Well, I've got evening surgery," she said.

"I meant—"

"I know," she interrupted with a smile.

"I mean, it doesn't look as if there can be any connection with the charity as they weren't involved in all of the cases."

"Although they were with some," Callie answered. "And it made me wonder if the killer could be getting their victims in more than one way."

"Like what?"

"Like from more than one charity, or from Hastings Care and the charity, I don't know. We really need to look at any connections, even if it's only between two of them. Then if we can find two organisations in common, we can look and see if anyone worked at both. Do you think Joyce will hand over the contact details?"

"Not if she gets legal advice. They will tell her not to release them without a warrant."

"And will you be able to get one?"

"I'm going straight back to try."

"You could try for one covering Hastings Care too, for their employee lists. Then we can see if there's any overlap."

"That's hardly likely, is it?"

"Why not?"

"You'd think someone whose day job was caring for the elderly wouldn't be likely to do it in their free time too, and anyway, if it's someone from the care team, they've visited all of the victims."

"No, Mrs Mount didn't have carers, nor did Mr Darling, just meals-on-wheels. Mrs Mount had a district nurse visiting and no, that's not the same thing. They might work out of the same building and for the same organisation, but they are all different teams."

"They could talk though, or even have access to records."

"True." Callie had to agree. "But we keep coming back to Mrs Friend dismissing the fact that her visitor was a carer. I'm sure she started to say that she was from the charity. Or a charity."

"And we've left her with them."

"We had no choice and we know it wasn't either of them because Mrs Friend didn't recognise their names." Miller had rung PC Adeola and got her to ask the old lady as soon they had left the office. "And there are two of them there. And one's a man." Callie went over all the arguments she had already put to herself when they set the arrangement up. Of course, it wasn't a perfect solution, but it was the best they could do under the circumstances.

"Okay," Miller conceded. "I'll try and get warrants for both AHC and Hastings Care and check the lists against each other, but if there is more than one way the killer is picking his victims, we might need to look at other potential sources."

"Like what?"

He thought for a moment before replying.

"Like church groups, doctors' surgeries, or taxi firms."

As she drove back to the surgery, Callie had to admit he had a point. She felt frustrated: the list of potential suspects was getting longer, not shorter, and it was only a matter of time before the killer would strike again. Of that, she was sure.

\* \* \*

Callie was still thinking about how the killer was finding their victims as she drove home after her evening surgery.

She thought, or hoped, that they could rule out the taxi firms, churches, and even the charity once she had realised that none of them were common with all the cases. But if the killer was involved with more than one of them, then that opened all those options up again.

"It means Miller will have to look at every one of them again," she explained to Billy, as she stirred what she hoped would pass for a marinara sauce while he prepared a salad to go with their simple pasta meal. The trouble was, nothing that seemed to be simple ever turned out to be as easy as Callie imagined it should be.

"That's a massive task."

"And that's supposing he can even get proper lists from them – I mean, churches don't keep databases of volunteers, generally."

In fact, she had no idea whether churches did or not, but she felt fairly sure that there was a good chance they wouldn't or, at least, that they wouldn't be kept up to date with any great regularity.

"Perhaps if they only check organisations that crop up more than once," Billy suggested. "That might cut it down a bit."

Callie thought about it. Hastings Care and the charity both figured several times but they hadn't found a taxi firm or church that cropped up more than once, as far as she knew. She would have to check with Miller.

Of the doctors' surgeries, Alan Darling was with Caroline Stratton's surgery, Mrs Mount from Angus McPhail's, Marek Bartosz from Dr Richardson's and Dolly Friend was with Callie's. One from each of the main practices in Hastings, although there was a connection between two in that Angus and Caroline were married, but they had been the first to point out the possibility of something criminal going on.

No, Callie couldn't see a connection between doctors, churches or taxi firms. If it was two sources, then it had to be the charity and Hastings Care. She just hoped that Miller managed to get their lists and find a name in common, because otherwise, they really weren't any further forward and would just be waiting around for the next victim to be targeted.

# Chapter 30

Callie had set her alarm deliberately early, much to Billy's disgust, because she wanted to check on Mrs Friend before work and see if she had said anything useful to Joyce or Derek, like the name of whoever was visiting her and supposedly sending her on holiday.

As she expected, she found the old lady already up, albeit in a pink housecoat and fluffy slippers, drinking tea with Derek Parsons, who was freshly shaven, impeccably dressed and squeaky clean. Quite a feat at that time of day, Callie thought. A blanket was folded on the armchair on top of a couple of pillows, suggesting that the helpers had slept, or dozed, in the sitting room overnight, making Callie feel even more guilty for having had a good night's sleep in her own bed.

"We're all awake and getting ready to face the day," Derek said cheerfully, getting a suspicious look from Mrs Friend in response. "Joyce is just getting dressed. I'll leave you two to it, while I just, er, use the facilities." He said and headed into what Callie assumed was the bathroom.

"I don't know who he is," Mrs Friend said in a stage whisper before Derek had even got to the door.

"He's from the charity," Callie told her, resisting the urge to whisper as well. "You know? The Ada Holmes Charity? He's here with Joyce to keep you company."

"No, he can't be," Mrs Friend insisted. "They don't come any more. They've closed down."

"No, you cancelled them," Callie told her. "They are still running and are willing to come back and help you. I think that would be a good thing, don't you?"

Callie looked up and saw Joyce coming out of a door at the back of the small flat. Like Derek she was up and dressed, but her clothes were crumpled and her hair was even messier than normal. The combs seemed to be doing very little to hold it in place.

"Of course," Joyce said and came into the room. "We can get someone to visit you as often as you need, Dolly, if you would like that?"

Mrs Friend looked around the room and then at Joyce.

"I don't know who she is," she said in a confidential voice and nodded towards Callie. "I don't know who any of you are, but I have to get ready because I'm going away." And with that, she got up and went into her bedroom.

Joyce gave a sigh and came and sat down. She looked understandably tired and more than a little frustrated.

"She's completely fixated about going away. It's the one thing she seems to be able to remember."

"She hasn't told you who her mysterious visitor is?"

"No, although I think she does know more than she is saying, but also remembers that she's been told not to say anything."

"Which is a shame."

"Yes, indeed."

"And it was definitely Mrs Friend who cancelled her visits from you?"

"Well, the volunteer who visited her told us and then I spoke with Mrs Friend to confirm." Joyce shifted in her chair and looked uncomfortable. "I did try and persuade her to keep us on, offered to find a different visitor if that was the problem, but she was adamant she no longer needed us, that she had family to care for her."

"But she hasn't."

"Well, no, I realise that now."

"And who was it who volunteered here?"

Joyce hesitated again.

"I've been thinking about this all night, and I telephoned our volunteers to ask their views. They have all given me permission to reveal their details," she paused, "except one. I haven't been able to get hold of her. Of course, she might be away or at work."

"And this is the lady who visited Mrs Friend?"

Joyce nodded before adding, reluctantly, "And she visited Mrs Mount, too, before Jean Lovejoy took over. She wasn't very happy at that, but Jean only lived round the corner, so it seemed sensible."

"But she didn't visit Mr Darling?"

"No."

Callie realised that Derek had come into the room.

"I visited Mr Darling," Derek said. "Went to him for years, apart from when my own mother was too sick, just before she died. Do you remember?" He looked at Joyce.

"Oh yes, I'd forgotten that."

"Did someone else visit then?"

"No one regular, unfortunately," Joyce told her.

"It's so unsettling for old people when they don't have the same person," Derek said, "but I couldn't leave Mum."

"And did the person who visited Mrs Mount and Mrs Friend ever fill in for you with Mr Darling?" But Callie already knew the answer to that from the anxious expression on Joyce's face.

"Well, yes, yes she did."

\* \* \*

After that, it hadn't taken a lot of persuasion for Callie to get Joyce to give her the name and telephone number of the volunteer in question. She had also promised to pop into the office and get any additional information they had stored there. There was no doubt in Callie's mind now that this volunteer was in some way involved, and, despite her protests, Joyce seemed to realise that there was some cause for concern.

"If she isn't involved, and I'm sure she isn't, then it's all just a coincidence, in which case you'll be able to clear it up pretty quickly, won't you?" she had babbled, but the look in her eyes told Callie that she had her suspicions about the woman, and Derek was looking uncomfortable too.

Callie was on the phone to Miller as soon as she left the flat.

"Steve?" she said as soon as he picked up. "I have a name for you, visited at least three of the victims – Ellie Thompson. Joyce is going to get her full contact details for you, but I have her mobile number here. She's not answering the phone and Joyce has already left a couple of messages for her. I'll check with my contact at Hastings Care and see if she's known to them."

But, much to Callie's disappointment, she wasn't.

* * *

Callie tried hard to concentrate on work throughout the morning, but found it almost impossible. She desperately wanted to know how the police were getting on with locating Ellie Thompson. She also wanted to know more about her and had tried everything she could to find her online. There were any number of Ellie Thompsons on Facebook, LinkedIn, Twitter and Instagram, and it would take ages for Callie to sift through them all, looking for anyone associated with Hastings. A quick trawl, which was all she could manage between patients, didn't reveal any likely contenders; she would need to do a more detailed search later on. Of course, some people weren't on any of those sites, but Callie didn't know many and was sure she would find her somewhere. Unless she had used a different name, maiden name, family name, nickname, because Callie knew all too well you could be called whatever you wanted online. She just hoped Miller was having more luck with the details that Joyce would have been able to supply; after all, the charity wouldn't let just anyone volunteer for them. Callie was certain that there would have to have been some sort of check on potential helpers.

As soon as surgery had finished, she called Miller, but there was no answer and she left a message. She then tried Detective Sergeant Jayne Hales.

"Can't talk to you now, Callie, we're busy trying to track down this Thompson woman."

"She's not at home?"

"Hasn't lived there for years, apparently. It was her parents' place. She moved out when she went to university, but moved back in to look after her mother when she was dying, according to neighbours. Lovely woman, very caring, so they say."

Whilst she was pleased that they were all busy trying to find this woman, curiosity was getting the better of Callie. She had to know more.

In the office, she set about doing a more detailed search under the name, but it was hopeless; none of the Ellie Thompsons she found seemed to be from Hastings, or rather the only one that she did find was still at school, so Callie felt able to discount her. She then tried variations on the name, such as Ella, Elinor, Elena, Eleanor or Elle, but again, no one stood out and none of the photos seemed familiar. Callie had to admit that she had no way of knowing if any of these people were serial killers, but she could say that none of them seemed likely to be. She gave up in despair and tried ringing Miller again. Failing there, she tried Joyce.

"Hi, it's Dr Hughes. Just calling to check all's well with Mrs Friend? Would you like me to come round and sit with her for a while? Give you and Derek a break?"

Predictably, Joyce leapt at the chance.

# Chapter 31

When Callie got to the estate where Mrs Friend lived, there were no parking spaces left at the front, so she drove around the back and left her car by the garage block, hoping that the area wasn't reserved for residents only. It was hard to tell, because the sign informing the public of the parking rules had been covered in black spray paint. Presumably by somebody angry at having fallen foul of them. She didn't want to put a "Doctor on call" sign on the dashboard because it might invite hopeful addicts to break into the car looking for drugs, or anything of value they could trade for drugs. It was that sort of estate.

There were two entrances into the lobby of the block of flats, both kept locked but with an intercom system for residents to buzz people in at the front. Only residents who knew the door code were supposed to use the back entrance. Callie suspected half of Hastings knew the code, no matter how frequently it was changed, and it didn't really matter because the door was often left propped open for deliveries, friends or customers to come in without disturbing anyone. Rather than walk around to the front, Callie thought she would check the back door first as she was closer to it. Sure enough, it was wedged open with some flyers from a local pizza delivery company.

She pulled the flyers free and closed the door behind her, aware of the hypocrisy of her actions: using the open door herself while denying others the chance. She knew it wouldn't be long before someone wedged it open again, but at least the block would be more secure for a short while.

The door to Mrs Friend's flat was opened by Derek almost as soon as she knocked.

"Have to feed the cats," he said as he hurriedly pulled on his coat and almost ran to the front door of the building.

"He's devoted to his cats," Joyce explained once Callie was inside. "All six of them. Now, PC Adeola, who was here this morning, was called out to a car fire just down the road. She said she wouldn't be long, so I'll stay until she or Derek gets back, shall I?"

"No, you go. I'll be fine."

"Are you sure?"

"Of course, I've brought a sandwich for my lunch and some cakes, so Dolly and I can have a cup of tea. Where is she?"

"Packing." Joyce rolled her eyes. "She seems to have everything bar the kitchen sink piled up and keeps trying to fit it all into her suitcase." She smiled, but still hesitated. "I don't like to leave you in case she comes."

"That's not likely, is it?" Callie insisted. "What with police cars driving by so often and Abi will be back shortly anyway. And they've probably picked up your Miss Thompson already."

"Mrs. She's married," Joyce said. "That much was in her volunteer file."

"She has a husband?" Callie wasn't sure why this hadn't occurred to her.

"Yes, although," Joyce hesitated, "I did wonder if they'd split up or something. Not that she ever said, but just that she never mentioned him, and caring for a relative can put a great strain on a relationship. Any relationship." She sounded as if she was speaking from personal experience. "You know, I still can't quite believe she has anything to do with this."

"Don't worry. If she hasn't, then it will all be cleared up once she speaks to the police." Callie tried to reassure the manager. "Do go. I feel guilty enough about having involved you and Derek already. You've done so much – let me take over here for a while. You never know, I might even get Mrs Friend talking."

"Well, I do need to go to the shop down the road. We're out of milk and we didn't want to go out for more, considering what you said about always being two of us. Are you sure you don't want me to wait for PC Adeola to come back?"

"Oh," Callie looked at the teacups she had already put out, "no, I'll be fine, it's only for a minute or two and it was more for Mrs Friend's protection I said that than anything else. You go and I'll wait to make the tea. There's a shop about two hundred yards along the road, towards town; I'm sure they will have milk."

"I saw it when I parked. I won't be long," Joyce said with a smile as she put on her coat, calling out: "Just nipping out for some milk, Dolly, but Dr Hughes is here."

It was hard to hear exactly what Dolly said in response, but Callie thought she heard, something about "wasteful" and "greedy" and it didn't sound in a friendly way.

"Derek has to have a bowl of cereal in the morning, apparently," Joyce confided and nodded at a jumbo size box of bran flakes which probably explained the length of time he had spent in the bathroom earlier. "Used the best part of a pint of milk, much to Dolly's disgust, although she said it was just as well as she wouldn't be needing it where she was going."

Relieved of her anxiety about leaving Mrs Friend, Joyce left. Once she had gone, Callie went in search of the elderly lady, finding her in the small back bedroom surrounded by a motley collection of clothes, books and photograph albums.

"How's it going?" she asked.

"Nearly there," Mrs Friend said, although the suitcase on the bed appeared empty apart from her slippers. "I'm not really sure what I should take."

"Well, that depends on where you are going, doesn't it? Is it somewhere hot?"

"It might be." She tried to think of the name of the place she was going but failed. "It's a lovely place for people my age. You get properly looked after, and they have nice plain food, nothing too fancy."

"That sounds wonderful, but if it's hot, some cool clothes would be a good idea; summer skirts and dresses, but a cardy for the evenings in case it gets chilly."

Inspired by this, Mrs Friend started putting some things in the case.

"Sandals maybe?" Callie suggested helpfully and these were added to the case. "Medication?"

Mrs Friend added a variety of pills and potions. Callie didn't think the small case would take much more.

"Will it take long to get there?" Callie continued fishing.

"Might do." Mrs Friend thought for a moment. "You need injections."

So that was how she was getting them to sit still and let her give them their fatal injection, Callie thought to herself. It was such a simple deception and none of the victims were knowledgeable enough, or clear thinking enough, to realise that travel injections were not given into a vein.

Callie asked a few more questions but Mrs Friend seemed to think she had said enough.

"I've got to get on, why don't you leave me alone?" she said brusquely and returned to her packing, adding a packet of biscuits to the case after a bit of thought.

"I'll make us tea then. Joyce will be back with the milk soon," she told Mrs friend, "and I have some cakes."

Mrs Friend brightened at that news; she was clearly partial to a cake.

"I hope they haven't got currants in," she said. "Currants give me wind."

Callie went into the kitchen and was making the tea and putting the cakes onto a plate, pleased to note that she hadn't bought anything with currants in, when the doorbell rang.

Before Callie could stop her, Mrs Friend had rushed into the hall and buzzed the main door open.

"You shouldn't do that, Mrs Friend. It could be anybody."

"It'll be her."

Callie sincerely hoped it wasn't and that it was Joyce back with the milk.

There was a tap on the door and Callie moved firmly past Mrs Friend and opened it, expecting to see Joyce standing there, but it wasn't. It was Eleanor Sweeting.

"Eleanor!" Callie said, shocked to see her trainee, or ex-trainee.

"She's trying to stop me going, Ellie, but I'm not going to let her," Mrs Friend shouted and tried to push Callie out of the way.

Ellie/Eleanor looked towards the front entrance where, through the glazed panels, Joyce and Abi Adeola could be seen walking towards the door, chatting and laughing, unaware that anything was going on. Making a quick decision, she headed for the back door.

"Eleanor! Wait!" Callie moved forward, but was stopped by Mrs Friend who was equally determined to reach her visitor.

"Ellie!" she called out and there was a bit of a struggle in the doorway as both of them tried to go after her.

The front door buzzer sounded and Callie gave up on going after Ellie and instead let the police woman and care manager in.

"She was here!" Callie urgently said to them both. "She went out the back way."

Adeola quickly realised what had happened and charged towards the back door, speaking into her radio as she went, calling for back-up. Callie handed Mrs Friend to Joyce and headed out the front door in case Eleanor doubled back towards the main road. She looked in both directions and even crossed the road to check there, but there was no one in sight. Well, there were lots of people, but no Eleanor Sweeting or Ellie Thompson, or whatever she was calling herself.

PC Adeola appeared from behind the building and looked at Callie. She shook her head. Eleanor had gone.

# Chapter 32

Callie sat in Miller's office, exhausted after what had turned out to be a very eventful day. She was trying to piece together everything she knew and had heard in the evening incident room briefing.

Once they knew that Ellie Thompson and Eleanor Sweeting were one and the same person, it had proved much easier to trace her. Thompson had been her married name but the couple were separated. There was no divorce listed anywhere, so presumably they were still married if not living together. Stuart Thompson worked in finance in Brighton and had no idea where his wife was living or what she was currently doing. She'd qualified as a doctor in Brighton, where they had met, but she had decided to come back to Hastings and look after her mother after only a few years of marriage.

"It was over anyway," he had told Miller. "She was obsessed with having a baby, wanted to throw good money after bad with endless IVF that the NHS wouldn't pay for, even though she worked for them. I'd had enough."

They hadn't kept in touch.

The address Ellie had given Joyce, and the GP training scheme, was her mother's house, and she had, of course, passed all the DBS and other checks in place with that address. However, after her mother's death, and once probate had been passed, it had been sold. Unfortunately, Ellie/Eleanor hadn't told anyone that, or updated them with her new address.

"She must have been watching the place this morning, and once she saw everyone leave, thought she was safe to visit Mrs Friend. She didn't know I was there because I'd come through the back," Callie told Miller when he came in and sat down after dismissing the team for the night.

"She probably set that car on fire to get Abi called away," he agreed. "She really is a piece of work."

"Yes. I rang Dr Richardson," Callie was beginning to feel overwhelmingly tired, "we have to put June Dingwall back on the list of victims."

"I thought she really was going away with her niece."

"That's what Eleanor told me, but Dr Richardson has confirmed that she doesn't – or rather didn't – have a niece. That's why he'd looked at me so strangely when I said it," she said, half to herself, "and you can stop looking for who went to the press. It was him. He thought we were disbanding the investigation, or not taking it seriously enough, anyway. And Mr Bartosz was his patient too, that's why he said four victims."

"When she moved from his practice to yours, did her day off change?" Miller asked.

"Yes." Which explained why the day of the murders changed as well. "I really should have spent more time listening to him, and not been blinded by Eleanor's description of him as a misogynist and a bully," Callie said with a rueful smile.

"Hindsight is a wonderful thing."

"Isn't it just." She yawned; it really had been a very long day.

"Can I tempt you to a drink?" Miller asked her.

"Sorry, I just want to crawl into my bed." She yawned again and closed her eyes.

"Alone?" Jeffries asked, startling her awake. Why did he always appear at the most inopportune moment and make the most inappropriate remarks?

"Yes," she snapped back. "Very definitely alone." Was it her imagination or did Miller look a tiny bit disappointed?

"Got a possible sighting, Guv," the detective sergeant said to Miller. "Near the pier. A unit thinks they saw her, but lost sight almost immediately."

"Thinks?"

"Their words, Guv, could be nothing but−" Jeffries shrugged.

Miller stood and grabbed his jacket off the back of the chair.

"No," he said firmly as Callie stood up as well. "You go on home, it's almost certainly a wild goose chase."

"And you'd only get in the way if it isn't, doc," Jeffries added, knowing full well that it would wind her up. He really was an odious little man, but Miller was right; she needed to go home and sleep.

* * *

She parked her car across the lane from her home, where the road widened and there was a little patch of gravel for that purpose. The chance of a parking spot was one of the reasons she had bought the flat − that and the uninterrupted views across the Old Town from her living-room windows. Her house was the last on the lane, beyond it, there was only the country park and finally, the cliffs. It had seemed idyllically quiet when she had bought the place, but sometimes when she got back late, like tonight, it seemed more isolated than quiet and secluded, as the estate agent had described it.

She could see a chink of light through the curtains of the ground-floor windows, so presumably someone was in there, but the rest of the house, and the house next door, were in darkness. Not for the first time, she thought that getting a dog might be a good idea.

As she walked up the path to the side door that led to the stairs up to her flat, the security light came on. She pulled out her keys, but before she could let herself into the building there was a rustle in the bushes. She turned and saw Eleanor, with a large knife in her hand.

"Open the door," she said and jabbed the knife at Callie who had frozen, keys in hand.

Callie took a moment to weigh up her options. She could chuck the keys at Eleanor and run for it, but Eleanor now stood between her and the road, and if she rushed through the shrubbery into the country park, she was likely to break her ankle in a rabbit hole or fall into a gorse bush. Eleanor was also younger and quite possibly fitter than Callie, so she would probably be able to outrun her. Screaming or calling for help would be an option, if the lady in the downstairs flat was not notoriously deaf and the man in the middle one was so clearly out, as the lack of lights and loud music testified. Who was there to hear her if she did scream?

"You've no choice – now open the door," Eleanor added as she watched the various thoughts flash through Callie's mind. Callie held up the keys in her hand to signify her agreement and opened the door.

"Go up the stairs."

Callie did as she was ordered, using the movement to hide the fact that she was checking in her pocket for her phone. It was there and switching it on wouldn't be a problem, but putting in her pin code and calling for help without being able to see what she was doing was going to be much harder. If she was in a television programme she'd be able to do it, but she wasn't sure she could in real life.

Once they were in Callie's flat, Eleanor made her sit down and then sat in the chair opposite so that she could watch her. Callie once again thought through her options. There was no chance that she would be able to fiddle with her phone without Eleanor realising what she was doing, but at least she wasn't in immediate danger. There was a coffee table between them and the few seconds that it would take Eleanor to get round it would give Callie the chance to run, but run where? Eleanor was closer than she was to the door and to the bedroom. Callie could only get to the kitchen area of the open-plan room before Eleanor. Even then, she would be on the wrong side of the breakfast bar, unable to easily reach over to get a knife out of the drawer or, better still, a frying pan from the cupboard. She was closer to the windows, but it was too big a jump onto the road two stories below. If she smashed the window, it almost certainly wouldn't get any attention as there was no building opposite, just a steep, bramble-covered drop, and her house was the last on the road, so only walkers passed by, not cars, and who would be out walking in the dark?

"Trying to work out an escape route?" Eleanor asked, correctly guessing her thoughts. "Don't bother. I checked the area out. It's very good of you to live somewhere so quiet."

As she discounted all these options Callie could feel panic rising, she took a deep breath and told herself that staying put and trying to talk Eleanor down was her best bet.

"Why did you come to me?" she asked in a slightly shaky voice. "At the LMC meeting."

"It was a shock to find out you were suspicious. I needed to keep an eye on you, find out what you were doing."

"Didn't help, though, did it?"

"No. I knew you were a meddling bitch, but I had no idea quite how much of one you were."

"Why did you do it?" Callie asked.

"Do what?"

"Kill those people."

"Put them out of their misery, you mean. Think of it as mercy killing."

"Mercy killing? They didn't want to die, any of them, and the way you did it? There was no mercy there, they all died in horrific pain."

Eleanor flushed, that barb had clearly hit home.

"I wanted it to be nice, peaceful even," she said. "Perhaps I should have added a painkiller into the injection, a barbiturate maybe, but they are so much harder to get. Potassium chloride was easy to get. I pocketed a few ampoules when I visited a parenteral nutrition lab as part of my training. Because they use it in euthanasia, I thought it would be painless."

"Well, perhaps you should have done more research."

"I wanted them to be happy." Eleanor stubbornly continued to try and justify her actions.

"That's why you pretended they were going away?"

"Yes, I wanted them to die looking forward to something. I'm not a monster. I didn't want them to suffer."

"But they did."

There was a sulky silence from Eleanor.

"Was it because of your mother? You wanted to get your revenge?"

"Revenge? Don't be silly. Like I said, I did it to end their misery."

"Except they weren't miserable. Some of them were quite happy."

"They don't know what they were!" Eleanor was angry now. "They didn't know if it was Christmas or Easter."

"They were confused." Callie tried to remain calm and dial back the anger. "And they were old, but is that reason enough to end their lives?"

"They were a drain on the NHS, on social services. All of them! They contributed nothing to the world and yet they had money thrown at them! Our money. Money that

could have been used elsewhere for people who are still—"
She struggled for the right word.

"Young?" Callie suggested.

"Useful members of society," Eleanor corrected her.

She closed her eyes for a moment, allowing Callie to reach for her mobile phone. She successfully switched it on and swiped to bring up the pin number entry page, keeping her eyes on Eleanor the whole time.

"I cared for my mother," Eleanor said quietly, "but by the end we needed daily carers to help me get her up."

Callie risked a quick glance and put in her pin number, before Eleanor opened her eyes again.

"Even though she could barely remember me, or who she was, when she developed heart problems, they sent her for a TAVI. Not just a routine valve replacement but a TAVI! Do you know what they cost?"

Callie did indeed know that a transcatheter aortic valve implantation procedure was notoriously expensive, but it was really the only safe way to replace heart valves in the frail elderly.

"She was probably too weak to withstand the normal procedure."

"Of course she was! But why were they replacing her valve at all? She was in her eighties, for God's sake, needing round the clock care, which social services didn't have to provide because I did it. I gave up my career, my marriage, my chance to have babies, and what for? For someone who was going to die soon anyway."

"You are young. You'll get more chances to have a career, have babies even."

"No, you know you're wrong. It's over — I've missed my chance at everything."

Callie silently agreed that Eleanor's career was over, but that wasn't because of her mother; it was because she was a killer and a bad doctor to boot.

"You know they only pay for two rounds of IVF because there isn't enough money to go round?" Eleanor continued trying to justify her actions, oblivious to whether or not Callie agreed. "In some areas it's even less – one or none at all. And meanwhile, they waste so much money on the old, on people with nothing left to give. It's criminal!"

Eleanor looked out of the window to hide the tears that had sprung into her eyes. Tears of sadness or righteous indignation, Callie wasn't sure. She took the chance to look again at her phone. She was frustrated to see that it had timed out so that the pin number page was back on. This time she didn't bother to put in her PIN, just swiped at the emergency call button, and again once it queried her action. It was hopeless.

"The old have already done their bit for society. They deserve to be treated well."

"That's rubbish and you know it. You agree with me really, I bet—" Eleanor turned and saw Callie look down briefly to check that the call was going through.

"What are you doing?" Eleanor jumped up and launched herself at Callie. Unable to even get out of her chair in time, all Callie could do to protect herself was to quickly throw the phone across the room.

"You bitch!" Eleanor turned as she heard the clatter of the phone hitting the floor.

"Help! I need help!" Callie shouted. "High Wickham, last house, flat 3."

Callie desperately hoped that it had connected to the emergency services and that the line had remained open in spite of everything.

As Eleanor turned to look for the phone, Callie grabbed her wrist and twisted it as hard as she could in an effort to get her to drop the knife. Eleanor snatched her hand back, freeing herself. She quickly moved back out of Callie's reach and towards where the phone must have landed.

To Callie's horror, she could see that her hand had been cut by the knife as Eleanor had pulled away. Blood was pouring from the wound and Callie grabbed a cushion and held it against the cut, pressing hard to stop the bleeding.

"Help!" Callie shouted to anyone who might hear on the end of the phone and repeated her address, the distress in her voice obvious. "She stabbed me!"

"I didn't mean to, you stupid cow," Eleanor said as she searched in vain for the phone. "You shouldn't have tried to get the knife."

Callie hoped the phone had slid under a chair or, better still, a cupboard. She made a dash for the kitchen and got a tea towel to wrap around her bleeding and useless hand and to look for a weapon. She grabbed a frying pan just as Eleanor launched herself across the breakfast bar. Callie took a swing with the pan and hit her shoulder. Unfortunately, not on the arm which held the knife.

"Ow!" The pain of the blow seemed to enrage Eleanor further, but before she could do anything, they both heard a key in the lock and the door opening. Both of them froze.

"Hi, honey, I'm home!" Billy called up the stairs in a parody of American sitcoms.

"Billy, don't come up, get help!" Callie shouted. "She's got a knife!"

"Shut up! Shut up! Shut up!" Eleanor shouted over the top of this.

"Get help!" Callie shouted again in the hope that Billy would hear her as Eleanor ran round the breakfast bar and stabbed at Callie with the knife.

The space was narrow and confined and she couldn't get a good swing, but Callie used the frying pan to bat away the knife. Eleanor continued her assault, edging forward as she did so and Callie continued to defend herself, backing off until she could feel the sink against her back. She could go no further.

To her dismay, she could see that Billy had not heeded her instruction to stay downstairs and get help. He must have raced straight up the stairs and, as Callie once again hit out with the frying pan, Billy grabbed Eleanor from behind and pulled her away from his lover. Billy and Eleanor struggled and then they overbalanced and fell in a tangled mess on the floor. Callie tried to grab Eleanor and pull her off Billy, but it was hard in the confined space between the kitchen units. She was slipping in blood, and ignored it, believing that it must be from her hand, and pulled again at Eleanor's arm.

Eleanor rolled back, trying to free her knife hand. They simultaneously realised that the blood was coming from Billy. Under his leather jacket, his once white shirt was now stained with blood, and the stain was growing rapidly.

"Billy!" Callie cried out and rushed to him, oblivious to the danger from Eleanor, who was scuttling backwards, away from them, away from Billy, a horrified look on her face as she realised what she had done.

Callie found the hole where the knife had entered his abdomen and ripped the shirt so she could see the wound, it wasn't large, but it was deep and bright red blood was pulsating out of it. Arterial blood.

"Pressure!" Billy gasped and Callie grabbed some clean tea towels from a drawer and pushed them hard against the wound, using her good hand.

"We need an ambulance, now!" she shouted as loud as she could in the hope that her phone was still connected to the emergency services. "Eleanor, call for an ambulance!"

But Eleanor was sitting, back against the wall, sobbing, the knife on the floor beside her, forgotten.

"Eleanor, you have to help me! Now!" Callie shouted and finally got through to the doctor. Eleanor shuffled across to Billy, away from the knife.

"Here, press here." Callie told her, and Eleanor did as she was told, pressing on Billy's wound with as much strength as she could muster. At last, her training and instinct to save life rather than end it were coming to the fore.

Reasoning that looking for her own phone would take too long, Callie grabbed Billy's from his pocket and used his finger to open it, thankful that he didn't use a PIN like her. She called the emergency services, asking for an ambulance and the police, all the while making sure that Eleanor was pressing hard on the wound, which she was, as she cried and muttered to herself.

"I didn't mean it, I just wanted to explain, why did you make me do it?"

Once she was sure help was on the way, Callie stroked Billy's head, telling him it was going to be okay, but he seemed to be losing consciousness.

"Stay with me, Billy. I can't lose you now," she told him and silently prayed to a God she wasn't sure she believed in.

Finally, in the distance, Callie could hear sirens. Help was arriving at last. She hoped it wasn't too late.

# Chapter 33

The blue flashing lights seemed to be everywhere. Callie was in the back of an ambulance, helping the paramedic stabilise Billy. Not that she was much help, as her right hand was almost useless, partly because of the big dressing strapped onto the wound on her palm. Billy now also had a tight dressing on his chest and the paramedic had put a drip up and attached a blood pressure monitor, oximeter and connected ECG leads to the sticky pads on Billy's chest. There was nothing for Callie to do, so she held Billy's hand, willing him to live, and checked the monitors, again. Callie could see that his pulse was too fast and his blood pressure too low; they needed to get him to hospital now and she glanced anxiously at the paramedic as he finished his observations and wrote everything down meticulously, while she was willing him to hurry up.

Looking at her watch, again, Callie saw that, although it had felt like hours, the whole incident had taken less than thirty minutes from Eleanor threatening her on the doorstep to the police and ambulance arriving. They were lucky that her emergency call had connected, and the shouts for help heard by the dispatcher who, not knowing exactly what was going on, sent police, ambulances and a fire tender, just to make sure everyone who could possibly be needed was there. And they were still there, as Callie could see through the ambulance doors. Two police cars, a paramedic car, an ambulance and a fire engine, all with their blue flashing lights illuminating a small crowd of onlookers who had gathered to see what was going on.

She was about to ask the paramedic to hurry up so they could go when she saw Eleanor being led to a police car by two uniformed officers. They placed her in the back of the patrol car, one of them carefully making sure she didn't hit her head as she was placed in there and the door closed.

Miller appeared at that moment, peering into the ambulance, concern etched on his face.

"Are you okay?" he said to her.

"Yes," she said thickly, and then they both looked over at Billy, unconscious, with the paramedic leaning over him, checking his vital signs and speeding up the drip.

"We need to go," the paramedic said and nodded at his driver who moved Miller out of the way and closed the doors before climbing into the front of the ambulance.

"Strap yourself in," Callie was ordered and she tried but couldn't manage to do it one-handed. She felt like a child, accepting help to put her seat belt on.

Later, Callie could remember little of the nightmare rush to the emergency department in the ambulance. The paramedic was rightly concentrating on Billy's condition, and the driver was busy driving as fast as he safely could to get them to the hospital in time. Once they arrived, the doors were flung open by a member of the team who had been pre-alerted and was standing by, ready to whisk Billy off to resus, the room best equipped for acutely sick patients.

Callie was left to follow, but as she reached the room's door she was steered away by a nurse in scrubs.

"Let's get that hand seen to," he said and led her to a cubicle round the corner. Desperate as she was to know how Billy was doing, she also knew she had to let the experts get on with their jobs. She would only be in the way.

Miller finally found her, sitting in the waiting room, anxiously looking up every time a nurse or doctor walked by, desperately waiting for news on Billy's condition. Her hand had been sewn up and dressed and her arm was in a sling.

"How's the hand?" he asked as he took the seat next to her, glaring at a drunk who was snoring in a seat in the corner. The waiting room was unusually quiet, even for three in the morning, probably because of the number of police and security around; it tended to put people off.

"Fine, I was lucky, nothing vital was damaged."

Both knew the same couldn't necessarily be said of Billy. He'd been taken to theatre soon after he arrived, and there was no news as yet.

"If I'd thought for one moment—" he started to say.

"You couldn't have known, none of us could have. I mean, I still don't understand why she came after me."

"If it helps, she says she didn't mean to hurt you, or Billy. She just wanted to explain why she had done what she did. She seemed to think you would understand, and that you might even agree with her actions."

"She clearly didn't know me very well."

Miller smiled at this.

"No, I think we can safely say that."

The consultant surgeon came into the room. He was still in his scrubs, having hurried straight from the operating theatre.

Callie stood up quickly, her heart hammering inside her chest, trying to read his face.

He smiled.

"He's a very lucky young man," the surgeon said and Callie felt her knees buckle with the relief. Luckily, Miller was there to catch her.

# Epilogue

They were sitting on the bench at the top of the cliff, looking out over the sea. The sun was shining, and it was a perfect day, except...

"I have to go now," Billy said, and he stood. His brother was standing at the top of the steps, looking at his watch and shuffling from one foot to the other.

"I know – they won't hold the plane for you," she said bravely.

They both stood, and Billy pulled her into an embrace and a deep kiss.

"I'll call tonight, once I'm settled in." His voice was thick, and he seemed reluctant to let her go. Just as reluctant as she was to let him go. They kissed again and then there was a loud cough from his brother.

"Go," she said, "I'll be coming out to see you in a couple of weeks."

He nodded and pulled away from her before abruptly turning and hurrying towards his brother.

She watched as they went down the steps together, Billy still walking a little stiffly but otherwise seemingly none the worse for his injuries now. He turned just before he went out of view and gave a little wave, and then he was gone.

The long weeks of summer since the stabbing had been a lovely, peaceful interlude. Billy had been extremely lucky, the surgeon had told her. The arterial blood she had seen was from the common hepatic artery, which was bad enough, but the knife had missed his aorta by millimetres, and then there would have been nothing she could do to save him.

Callie had cared for Billy as he recuperated, shooing his family away when he was too tired to take their constant bickering and the mounds of food they always seemed to bring. Helping him to heal. But then the time had come. Professor Wadsworth hadn't apologised, in fact, he'd suggested in one report that it was he who had first alerted the police to the possibility of murder, but everyone knew that wasn't true. Well, everyone who mattered, both at the Home Office and in Northern Ireland, and the job offer was back on.

Billy had to make a decision: take up the post in Northern Ireland or return to work at the hospital here in Hastings. They had discussed it endlessly, and much as she didn't want him to go, Callie had known that he would always regret it if he stayed. They had agreed to try and continue their relationship in separate parts of the country for now, and decide in the future where to make their home. Together. Hopefully.

Callie sat back down on the bench and wiped away a tear. They had grown very close, and she would miss him terribly, but she was strong, independent, she would cope.

She sat for a while longer, but the evening was beginning to get cool. Summer was over, autumn had arrived.

What she needed was some company. And a drink. There was always Kate and The Stag.

She stood up and took out her phone.

"Hi, Kate, last one to the bar pays for the round," she said and hurried to the steps.

THE END

If you enjoyed this book, please let others know by leaving a quick review on Amazon. Also, if you spot anything untoward in the paperback, get in touch. We strive for the best quality and appreciate reader feedback.

editor@thebookfolks.com

www.thebookfolks.com

## ALSO IN THIS SERIES

*Available on Kindle and in paperback.*

DEAD PRETTY – Book 1

When a woman is found dead in Hastings, Sussex, the medical examiner feels a murder has taken place. Yet she feels the police are not doing enough because the victim is a prostitute. Dr Callie Hughes will conduct her own investigation, no matter the danger.

BODY HEAT – Book 2

A series of deadly arson attacks piques the curiosity of Hastings police doctor Callie Hughes. Faced with police incompetence, once again she tries to find the killer herself, but her meddling won't win her any favours and in fact puts her in a compromising position.

## GUILTY PARTY – Book 3

A lawyer in a twist at his home. Another dead in a private pool. Someone has targeted powerful individuals in the coastal town of Hastings. Dr Callie Hughes uses her medical expertise to find the guilty party.

## VITAL SIGNS – Book 4

When bodies of migrants begin to wash up on the Sussex coast, police doctor Callie Hughes has the unenviable task of inspecting them. But one body stands out to her as different. Convinced that finding the victim's identity will help crack the people smuggling ring, she decides to start her own investigation.

## MURDER LUST – Book 6

After noticing strange marks on the body of a woman found dead in a holiday let, police doctor Callie Hughes probes further. The police take her concerns about a serial killer seriously, but achieve little when another body if found. Callie is possibly the only obstacle to the murderer getting away with the crime, and that makes her a potential target.

*For more great books, visit www.thebookfolks.com*

Printed in Great Britain
by Amazon

31773766R00142